"Michelle and I broke up tonight."

"Well, don't feel too bad, Steve. You lasted longer than most of them." Janet thought to herself—Michelle had held onto Steve until after football homecoming. This gave her plenty of time to find another guy before the round of Christmas parties.

"She said she wanted to date other guys."

"Then I guess you can date other girls, Steve," Janet said unsympathetically.

"Yep, I suppose so. Only I'm not sure I want to."

"You're that hung up on Michelle?" Janet asked, feeling bitter.

"Oh, I don't know. Sure, she's a hard act to follow . . ."

You're telling me! Janet thought angrily.

Caprice Romances from Tempo Books

SMALL TOWN SUMMER by *Carol Ellis*
DANCE WITH A STRANGER by *Elizabeth Van Steenwyk*
TERRI'S DREAM by *Margaret Garland*
PINK AND WHITE STRIPED SUMMER by *Hazel Krantz*
A SPECIAL LOVE by *Harriette S. Abels*
SOMEONE FOR SARA by *Judith Enderle*
S.W.A.K. SEALED WITH A KISS by *Judith Enderle*
PROGRAMMED FOR LOVE by *Judith Enderle*
WISH FOR TOMORROW by *Pam Ketter*
THE BOY NEXT DOOR by *Wendy Storm*
TWO LOVES FOR TINA by *Maurine Miller*
LOVE IN FOCUS by *Margaret Meacham*
DO YOU REALLY LOVE ME? by *Jeanne R. Lenz*
A BICYCLE BUILT FOR TWO by *Susan Shaw*
A NEW FACE IN THE MIRROR by *Nola Carlson*
TOO YOUNG TO KNOW by *Margaret M. Scariano*
SURFER GIRL by *Francess Lin Lantz*
LOVE BYTE by *Helane Zeiger*
WHEN WISHES COME TRUE by *Judith Enderle*
HEARTBREAKER by *Terry Hunter*
LOVE NOTES by *Leah Dionne*
NEVER SAY NEVER by *Ann Boyle*
THE HIDDEN HEART by *Barbara Ball*
TOMMY LOVES TINA by *Janet Quin-Harkin*
HEARTWAVES by *Deborah Kent*
STARDUST SUMMER by *Pam Ketter*
LAST KISS IN APRIL by *N. R. Selden*
SING A SONG OF LOVE by *Judith Enderle*
ROCK 'N' ROLL ROMANCE by *Francess Lin Lantz*
SPRING DREAMS by *Nola Carlson*
CHANGE OF HEART by *Charlotte White*
PRESCRIPTION FOR LOVE by *Judie Rae*
CUPID CONFUSION by *Harriette S. Abels*
WILL I SEE YOU NEXT SUMMER? by *Judith Enderle*
SENIOR BLUES by *Francess Lin Lantz*
NEW KID IN TOWN by *Jean Thesman*
A HARD ACT TO FOLLOW by *Charlotte White*
WANTED: A LITTLE LOVE by *Stephanie Gordon Tessler*

A CAPRICE ROMANCE

A Hard Act to Follow

Charlotte White

TEMPO BOOKS, NEW YORK

A HARD ACT TO FOLLOW

A Tempo Book / published by arrangement with
the author

PRINTING HISTORY
Tempo Original / September 1984

ISBN: 0-441-31711-1

Tempo Books are published by The Berkley Publishing Group,
200 Madison Avenue, New York, New York 10016.
Tempo Books are registered in the United States Patent Office.
PRINTED IN THE UNITED STATES OF AMERICA

Chapter One

The cloud of pink chiffon swirled and billowed before Janet's eyes until she grew dizzy.

"What do you think?" Michelle asked excitedly as she stopped twirling. Her blue eyes were fixed on her sister's face as she waited for her reaction.

"Great, Michelle," she mumbled, knowing she sounded as unenthusiastic as she felt. "All pink and fluffy, just like cotton candy."

Michelle hurried toward the mirror and peered anxiously into it. "Oh, Mom," she wailed, "maybe it is too much. Do you think so?"

Shaking her head in disgust, Janet stuck her hands in her pockets and moved closer to the door. "No, I don't, Michelle," replied their mother, giving Janet a reproving look. "It's very lovely and feminine. The dress is perfect for you." She turned then and addressed Janet directly, "It wouldn't hurt you, you know, to give your sister a sincere compliment once in a while."

Janet shrugged. "I said it was great, didn't I? What more do you want from me?" Before either of them had a chance to answer, she added, "I'm going downtown for a few minutes. Is it okay if I take the car?"

"I suppose so," Nancy Lindquist said, "only don't be gone too long. The new neighbors are coming for dinner tonight, remember. You need to allow time to clean up and change your clothes."

"What's the matter . . . ?" Janet began, her brown eyes flashing with indignation.

"Don't argue," Nancy interrupted firmly. "It won't hurt you to look nice the first time you meet them. You are to wear one of those pretty sundresses I bought you. And that's the final word."

Janet left without another word, closing the door behind her firmly enough to show her irritation—but not so hard that her mother would get mad. Having just turned seventeen, she had figured out just how far she could push her parents.

Settling herself in the driver's seat of the station wagon, Janet breathed a sigh of relief. She really didn't have to go to town, but she definitely needed to get out of the house. Why, she thought in irritation, did Michelle need another new formal, anyway? One entire side of her closet was packed with long dresses, most of them worn only once. It wasn't as if she were running for a beauty contest. What was left? She had already won all the contests. Riding down Main Street on a float as Miss Sloan County did not mean that Michelle needed a gown that no one had seen before. It was ridiculous.

Janet shook her head in near disgust as she turned the key in the ignition. "Wear one of those pretty sundresses," she muttered under her breath, mocking her mother in a way that was not exactly respectful—although it did let her get rid of the excess steam she had built up. So the new neighbors were coming over. Big deal. And so what that they had a teenage boy who—from a distance, anyway—looked like quite a hunk. Janet knew she could wear anything from a formal gown to a bikini and no one would notice. Not when Michelle was there. That was the way it always had been and always would be.

Parking the car, she got out and put a quarter in the meter, then sauntered into the drugstore. She was staring at the magazine rack when the clerk asked, "May I help you, Janet?"

Janet turned to face Emily McClellan, one of Michelle's friends. The girl was well dressed and perfectly groomed, making Janet acutely aware of her own faded jeans and T-shirt. She had been so eager to get away from the house that she had not even looked in the mirror. Probably, she thought, she had pizza sauce on her nose and the mass of reddish curls that topped her head were even more tangled than usual. But what did she care? she thought defiantly. She wasn't trying to look like a model. Squaring her shoulders, she looked Emily right in the eye. "No, thanks, Em. I just want something to read, but I think I can find it on my own."

"Okay—just let me know if you need help. By the way, we did get some new paperbacks in."

"Fine."

Emily kept standing there. Janet wished she would go away.

"Where's Michelle today?"

"Home. She's trying on her dress for the county fair parade Saturday."

"Oh, yeah? Did she get the one from Nicole's?"

"I don't know," Janet muttered ungraciously. "It's pink. That's all I know. Pink like Pepto-Bismol."

Emily surprised Janet by giggling. "Pepto-Bismol, huh? That's pretty cute, Janet."

Her pleasure in Janet's small joke seemed genuine, but Janet, a cynic by nature, wondered if Emily's appreciation was due to Janet's wit or to the fact that she had placed only third in the Miss Sloan County contest. Finally, seeing that she was not going to get rid of Emily easily, Janet picked out two paperback novels at random, paid for them, and left the store. There seemed to be no place to go to be by herself. She couldn't forget the image of Michelle happily modeling the long dress, and Janet couldn't figure out why. After all, it was not as if she were jealous. She didn't want to be like Michelle. Janet thought all these teen pageants and contests were ridiculous. She did not believe she could ever bring herself to twist and turn on stage in front of a bunch of people.

All that was true. But inside she knew she ached to be as pretty and as popular as her sister. And with an edge of bitterness, she realized she would never be any of those things. Michelle was Michelle and Janet was Janet. They were no more alike than if they had sprung from completely different planets. Crazy mixed-up genes, Janet thought wryly. It's like Michelle got all the good ones and when Janet came along a year later, she got the leftovers.

"Leftover genes," she wailed to herself in the car, imitating a country music singer. She grinned, thinking how dumb she must sound. Having nothing else to do, she gave a deep sigh, and headed toward home. Maybe things had calmed down now and the cotton candy gown had been put away until Saturday. She certainly hoped so.

"You look very nice, dear," Nancy Lindquist commented. "You should wear a dress more often."

Janet glanced down at the bright print of her sundress. "I feel like a pig in an Hawaiian print truss."

Her mother narrowed her eyes, letting Janet know her levity was not appreciated. "Just kidding," Janet murmured, turning up the corners of her mouth in a fake smile, keeping her lips pressed together.

"If you're going to smile, smile properly," commented her mother. "You have lovely teeth—be proud to show them."

Lovely teeth, Janet thought scornfully, knowing better than to say anything else. That was about the only lovely thing about her. And she only had that by the grace of two thousand dollars and three years of braces. Even now the metal retainer sat on her night table in its round plastic box, ready to be worn every night. Naturally, Michelle had not required orthodontic work.

"Do the Waymans only have one kid?" she asked, her mouth full of cheese-filled celery.

"Um, yes . . . that is, just one living here with them. Margaret told me they left two grown children behind when they moved to Wisconsin. And stay out of the food. It's for dinner. Besides, all that extra snacking puts on weight, you know."

"My gosh, Mom, it's celery. Celery doesn't even have calories, does it?"

"No, Janet, but cheese most certainly does." With a swift movement, she took a stalk from Janet's hand and returned it to the glass dish. "Go set the table. Make yourself useful instead of detrimental."

Janet gave an offended sniff. "Good china?"

"Yes, of course. And do be careful."

"Uh, Mom, why are we trying to impress the Waymans with the good china? Which have they got—money or social position? Or is it both?"

Nancy removed a hot dish from the oven and gave a deep sigh of exasperation. "I am not trying to impress anyone, Janet." Her words were very precisely spoken, a sure sign she was irritated. "I am merely trying to make a new family welcome in our neighborhood and community."

"Hey, cool it, Mom. It was just a joke. Don't overreact."

"There are times, dear, when your sense of humor goes too far. Now, go on and set the table."

Loudly singing a few bars of the latest AC-DC song, Janet headed toward the dining room. She could hear her mother sigh in disgust. Janet smiled to herself. She really did love her mother, but sometimes she couldn't resist bugging her.

As luck would have it, the front doorbell rang when no one else was in sight. Janet looked around helplessly. She hated playing hostess. Mom was busy in the kitchen and Dad was outside checking the charcoal, but where was Miss Sloan County? "Michelle?" she called loudly. There was no response. She probably was hiding out, preferring to make an entrance later on. Or maybe she wasn't finished putting makeup on her already perfect face. The doorbell rang again and Janet slammed down the pile of napkins in frustration.

There they stood: Mrs. Nerd, Mr. Nerd, and Sonny. . . . Well, Sonny sure didn't look like a nerd. He was even better looking close up.

"Uh, come on in," she said, letting her arms flap awkwardly against her sides. "Well, have a seat. Mom and Dad will be in here in just a moment."

They all sat down rather hesitantly, perching uncomfortably on the edges of their chairs. All of them looked at her as if they were expecting something. Panic was quickly rising within her. Where was everyone else? She was no good at this.

"Uh, you must be the Waymans." Absolutely brilliant conclusion, she thought. Who else would they be? The three dwarfs all dressed up, accidentally dropping by on their way back to the forest? The thought made her smile. That six-footer with the wavy brown hair was no dwarf.

"Yes, that's right," Mrs. Wayman said, obviously amused. "I'm Margaret and this is my husband, Bill, and our son Stephen."

"Well, uh, pleased to meet you. I'm Janet, the younger dwarf—er, I mean, Lindquist." Her face had flamed as soon as her tongue had slipped. How often had that happened to her? She would be thinking some absolutely nonsensical thing, and, before she knew it, she had said it.

Mrs. Wayman crossed her knees and primly pulled the double-knit dress down over them. She regarded Janet quizzically. From the corner of her eye, Janet saw Stephen put a hand up to his mouth to cover his smile. "Do you go to school in Barkley, dear?"

"Uh, yes. I'll be a junior."

"That's nice. Steve will be a senior."

"I see."

If the whole evening is going to be like this, I don't think I can stand it, thought Janet. She moved quickly toward the doorway. "I'll tell my folks you're here. Just make yourselves comfortable."

On the way to the kitchen, she caught sight of herself in the wall mirror. She had a blob of cheese on her throat. Angrily she picked it off. Who cared what she looked like anyway? Or how she acted, for that matter? If the Waymans didn't like her, well . . . well, they could go eat dinner elsewhere.

"Mom," she hissed as soon as she was in the kitchen, "they're here. You have to get in there."

"Oh, all right, dear. . . . Here, you watch the sauce. And keep stirring or it will scorch."

Janet was not often glad of the opportunity to work in the kitchen, but anything was preferable to trying to talk to the Waymans. She'd never been good at meeting new people. All too soon, however, Nancy reappeared in the kitchen.

"Go on back in and entertain them, Janet. I told them it would only be a few moments until I could leave the kitchen."

"I can't go back in there."

"Why on earth not?"

"I don't know what to say to them. It's very awkward."

"For heaven's sake, Janet. Don't make such a big deal out of it. You need to learn to make small talk. Now go on."

Feeling like she was being led to her execution, Janet went back to the living room. Her smile felt stiff and wooden. Now she had to think of something to say. Sitting down at one end of the couch, she searched her mind frantically.

"Your mother's a very nice lady, Janet," said Bill Wayman.

"Yeah, she's okay," Janet managed to reply. After all, what on earth was an appropriate response to a comment like that?

"And so young looking," Margaret Wayman added. "Why, I'll bet she could easily pass for your sister."

Janet smiled again, hoping the smile did not look as fake as it felt. Speaking of sisters, she thought, where was hers?

Michelle chose that moment to make her entrance. And that's exactly what it was. Michelle did not simply walk into the room—she made an entrance. Pausing for a moment, framed by the doorway, she smiled warmly. Anyone would assume Michelle was enchanted to see the Waymans. Her long, nearly black hair fell across her shoulders as soft and shining as velvet and her blue eyes looked enormous in her heart-shaped face. The simple white dress fitted her tall, slender frame as if it had been designed especially for her.

In contrast to the simplicity of Michelle's dress and smooth hair, Janet was even more aware of her own unruly curls and brightly colored dress. Suddenly Janet felt tacky.

"Hi," Michelle said and went right on to introduce herself to the Waymans as smoothly as if she were a charm-school graduate. All three pairs of eyes were on her. Strangely enough, Janet suddenly relaxed. Now it did not matter what she wore, or how much cheese she had on her neck. The spotlight was off her and she was enormously relieved.

It was amazing. Janet had seen it happen repeatedly and yet it never failed to amaze her. In four minutes flat, Michelle had established the following:

Mr. Wayman was an office manager in a textile manufacturing company. In his spare time he enjoyed golf, fishing, and penny-ante poker.

Mrs. Wayman was an R.N. and hoped to find part-time work. She crocheted, decorated fancy cakes, and played a mean hand of bridge.

They had two older married children and two small grandchildren.

Steve planned to contact the school as soon as possible so he could get in on the first football practice. At first, he had not wanted to move from his hometown, especially for his senior year, but he had gradually adjusted to the idea. Barkley was a larger town and he felt he might get in on some opportunities he had not had before. After graduation from high school, he planned to study computer science at a university specializing in engineering.

And all the information was gained with ease. Michelle and the three Waymans were soon chatting away like old friends. If she had tried to find out all that stuff, Janet thought, she would have sounded like a cross-examiner in a courtroom. Settling back against the couch, she sighed deeply. Preferring to go barefoot, she was bothered by any shoes and the sandals she was wearing were very uncomfortable. The silly things had no straps at all except a narrow one across the top of the foot. For the sake of nothing better to do, she wiggled her feet in the sandals until the right shoe fell off onto the carpet. Embarrassed, she bent to pick it up and slipped it back on. She was absentmindedly humming the same raunchy song she had sung for her mother's benefit.

Looking up suddenly, she saw that Steve was staring at her. His eyes were crinkled at the corners and the corners of his mouth were twitching. Realizing he must know the song she had been humming, Janet flushed, then shrugged and met his eyes. This time her smile was impish and real. This Steve character was certainly cute. Tall and ruggedly handsome with wavy hair and a cleft in his chin. What more could you ask for? And he was neatly dressed in new-looking jeans and a white terry shirt that contrasted gorgeously with his tan. He was the only one of the Waymans who did not seem to be wearing polyester. Polyester was one of Janet's chief prejudices in life. She absolutely hated the stuff. When she had been a little girl, her mother had made her pull-on-style stretch pants in a variety of colors. They all seemed to have one thing in common: they were all two sizes too big. When she finally outgrew them, it took a lot of persuasion to refrain her mother from making more. Since then, Janet had lived in jeans, but her hatred of that fabric had persisted.

"What's for dinner, Janet?" Michelle asked cheerfully, trying to draw her mute sister into the conversation.

Janet had not been expecting the question. "Polyester, I think," she blurted out. And immediately thought, There I go again.

Michelle laughed and Janet was instantly aware of the magic, lilting sound of her laughter. And so, she noticed, was Steve Wayman. His eyeballs were practically hanging out. Michelle had made another conquest. Janet wondered how many notches she had on her curling iron by now.

"You'll have to excuse my sister," Michelle told the Waymans. "She's a dreamer. When her mind is wandering, you never know what she'll say."

Janet was seething inside with resentment. Okay, so it was true and she had said something really dumb. Yet she still resented it that Michelle was apologizing for her, making it sound as if she were a half-wit of some sort.

"Really, Janet. I don't know about you," Michelle commented, shaking her head with an air of amused tolerance. "And what is for dinner—really?"

"Dad's charbroiling steaks and Mom's made a lot of salads and junk."

Nancy and Roger Lindquist both came into the room then, apologizing for the delay in greeting the Waymans. As they settled down to chat for a few moments before eating, they both were relaxed and friendly. Watching her parents and sister, Janet decided she should check out her family tree to see which ancestor had passed down the personality she had inherited. No doubt it was the same one who had fuzzy hair and freckles, a short stature, and rather sturdy legs. When she was younger, she had gone through a period of thinking she was adopted. When her parents were out of the house one day, she had desperately searched through the desk drawers for some clue to the adoption. Instead she'd found her birth certificate and a snapshot of her pregnant mother holding Michelle. She had been as much disappointed as relieved. It would have been a good explanation for her faults. Now all the blame had to rest on the crummy assortment of genes fate had passed her way.

"Janet informed us we were having polyester for dinner," Margaret Wayman said jokingly.

Nancy opened her mouth, then quickly closed it. She shot Janet a brief look of dismay. Being very aware of Janet's feelings about polyester, her sharp mind registered Bill's slacks and Margaret's dress. Knowing her daughter well, she realized exactly where Janet's mind had been. "Yes," she managed to say, "our younger daughter is quite a character."

"The two girls are so different," Margaret commented.

Janet sniffed rather loudly. She'd heard that comment before.

Finally it was time for dinner. With obvious pride, Janet's father served the steaks—each cooked according to each person's preference. Almost immediately, Janet began wishing the meal were over. Each time she cut off a piece of steak, her knife squeaked audibly across the plate. She wished they were having something simple to eat—like hot dogs or mashed potatoes. Even she could eat mashed potatoes well. They didn't crunch rudely like celery or slurp noisily like soup. Suddenly, her knife fell off her plate and dropped a spot of butter on the previously spotless tablecloth.

"Leave it to me," Janet said cheerfully.

"Usually I'm the first to spill something," Steve said kindly. "I'm glad you got the honors this time."

"I generally do," Janet quipped. "If they gave medals for messes, I'd be a five-star general by now."

"You only have two children, then?" Margaret asked Janet's mother. Janet wondered what had brought that on and felt she knew. Margaret was probably thinking that if she had a kid like Janet, she probably wouldn't take a chance on another one either.

"Yes," Mrs. Lindquist said with a gracious smile. "We had wanted a large family once. But the girls were so close in age and so lively when they were little that they kept us hopping. So we decided to stop at two."

"Do we have to discuss birth control *before* dessert?" Janet asked.

Nancy turned as red as her blouse. Michelle's large eyes grew even wider. Roger kept his head down and seemed suddenly quite interested in his scalloped potatoes. Margaret choked on her salad while Bill had a coughing spell. Meanwhile, Steve was laughing uncontrollably and was soon joined by Janet's father. Janet had never loved her father more than she did at that moment. If he had gone all stern and dignified on her, she knew she would have died.

Soon everyone else was treating it as a spontaneous joke. Their laughter seemed a bit nervous at first, but no one seemed truly offended. Janet had not realized she had been holding her breath until a long sigh of relief escaped her.

"Sorry," she said as the giggles subsided. "It just slipped out."

"You have quite a sense of humor," Margaret commented. "Do you go in for dramatics at school?"

Janet, who avoided school as much as possible, looked at Steve's mother. "Oh, not really," she said airily. "I'm not very interested in school activities."

"I see," Margaret said quietly. "Well, as I remarked earlier, Nancy—your two daughters are certainly different."

Seeing that her mother was trying to think of something appropriate to say, Janet came to her rescue. After all, the truth was the truth. "Yes," she said brightly, "it makes it kind of interesting, though. Having Farrah Fawcett and Groucho Marx under one roof. It's a wonder we don't charge for the floor show."

"Janet, you're incorrigible." To someone who didn't

know her well, Mrs. Lindquist didn't sound angry, but Janet knew better. After the Waymans left, she would get a long lecture about her behavior.

"In case you aren't sure," Janet added, "I'm Groucho Marx. Now, if you'll excuse me, I'll go check on dessert."

As she left the room, she bent over and walked like Groucho and, looking back, wiggled her eyebrows comically at her guests. Usually she did not bother to help in the kitchen unless she was forced to. This evening she just had to get out of that room.

For the rest of the evening, she managed to keep quiet and behave herself. She tried to look pleasant and kept her thoughts to herself. She watched her sister turn the full force of her considerable charms on Steve all evening, so it was no surprise when she heard Michelle and Steve make plans to go out the next night. Michelle had engineered the whole thing so skillfully that Steve probably thought he had asked for the date and felt grateful she had accepted.

When the guests had gone Janet excused herself, saying she didn't feel well. The lecture could wait until later. Maybe some of her mother's anger would have subsided by that time.

After the house was quiet, she tiptoed down to the kitchen and fixed herself a peanut butter sandwich. She felt more relaxed now that she was alone and had had a few hours' respite from the lecture.

As she passed her parents' bedroom door, she heard her name mentioned.

"Okay," Janet heard her mother say. "I see the funny side of it. But Roger, I didn't set out to raise a stand-up comedienne. And it can be terribly embarrassing the way Janet just blurts out anything. It's like having an overgrown four-year-old."

"Now, Nancy," Roger soothed. "Janet's just having some growing pains. And, to tell the truth, I rather enjoy her just like she is. I don't doubt that one day she'll go all silly and feminine on me, but right now . . ."

His voice became muffled and Janet went on to her room. She really did not want to hear herself discussed, anyway. Good old Dad. Maybe he would rescue her from the lecture—and maybe he wouldn't. Besides, it didn't really matter. What did another lecture matter, anyway?

Another year or so and she was going to go as far away from Barkley and everyone in it as she possibly could. Settling down on her bed, she pulled her stock of college brochures from the drawer of the nightstand. She picked one at random, opened it, and took a large bite of her sandwich. The location of the school did not matter, nor did the field of study. All that could be decided later. Right now the important thing was simply getting away—to a place where no one had ever seen or heard of Michelle Lindquist.

Chapter Two

"Hello," Janet said unenthusiastically. "Come on in, Steve." Leaving the front door wide open, she returned to her seat on the floor. Though she tried not to care, she couldn't help noticing how nice Steve looked in his crisp khaki pants and red polo shirt. Without a doubt, the new neighbor was good-looking. He was also Michelle's conquest, so what difference did it make to Janet what he looked like?

As usual, Michelle wasn't ready yet. It had always irritated Janet that her sister was never available to answer the doorbell or the telephone. Janet often felt like a combination doorman, butler, and receptionist. The feeling was not enjoyable. "She'll be ready pretty soon," Janet told Steve without looking up.

"Okay. What are you doing?"

Instead of sitting down and ignoring her, as Janet expected, Steve sat down beside her on the floor. Having him hover over her made her more than a little nervous.

"Enamel work," she replied shortly.

"Looks neat. How do you do it?"

Great, she said to herself, now he thinks he is obligated to be kind to Michelle's little sister—awful though she may be—and make polite conversation until Michelle decides to emerge in all her radiant glory.

"Well?" he asked again when Janet showed no signs of answering.

Sighing wearily, she picked up the round wooden disc she'd been working on and handed it to Steve. "After the design has been imprinted on the wood you start applying the enamel paint, using little brushes. Each layer of paint has to dry completely before you put on the next layer. You keep painting layers until you get the effect you want."

"Sounds time-consuming."

"It is—but I have plenty of time. My life is not exactly a whirl of social activities."

"Why not?"

Janet's irritation increased. She fought down the urge to throw one of the paint-covered brushes at him, marring his spotless appearance. Instead, she merely shrugged, not looking over at him.

"You trying to tell me there's not much demand for a female Groucho Marx in Barkley?"

She glanced at him quickly. His blue eyes were friendly and kind and she felt her hostility melt away.

"Not much," she admitted, giving him a grin to show she didn't care. "My kind has yet to be appreciated in the great metropolis of Barkley."

"Your day will come," he said.

Yeah, she thought cynically. If he thinks I'm so wonderful, why did he make a date with Michelle?

"So what do you do with these things when they're done?" he asked, returning his attention to her craftwork.

"If you'll turn it over, you'll see the inside is hollowed out. It's a lid; there's a deeper bottom part. I give them for Christmas gifts. They make good boxes for hair barrettes, rings, paper clips—any kind of odds and ends."

"Neat. Where do you get the wooden boxes?"

"Dad makes them for me—but I do the sanding and varnishing myself."

"Multitalented, huh? I'm impressed."

"I'll just bet you are. And that's just the beginning."

"Oh, is that right?"

"Definitely."

"What other talents do you have, Janet?"

"For starters, I tap-dance and juggle."

"Simultaneously?"

"Of course. Care for a demonstration?"

Before he could answer, Janet got up from the floor, took several pieces of wax fruit from the basket on the end table, and began madly throwing them up in the air while her feet moved rapidly in an exaggerated tap dance.

"Hey," Steve protested with a laugh when the fruit began to rain down on his head. "I think you better stick with the enamel work."

"You don't like my vaudeville routine?"

"Let's just say that the painting is less dangerous to bystanders."

"All I need is a bit of practice."

She picked up the fruit and tried again. When the apples and bananas began to fly, she and Steve were laughing so heartily that they did not see Michelle come into the room.

"Good grief," she said with lofty superiority. "What *are* you doing now, Janet?"

"Entertaining your date, sister. Since you're never ready, someone has to do it."

"Simple conversation would be sufficient."

"But definitely boring. If you don't like my act, then answer the doorbell yourself from now on."

She did not care if she sounded petty. Once Steve caught sight of Michelle in her pale-pink slacks and shirt, his face lit up and Janet knew he was no longer aware of her existence.

"Really, Janet, you're impossible." With an air of dismissal, Michelle turned away from her sister and addressed Steve. "Ready to go?"

"Sure."

He appeared almost in a daze as Michelle led the way to the front door. To his credit, he did not entirely forget that Janet was there. "Uh, see you, Janet," he mumbled, his eyes riveted on Michelle's face.

"Yeah, sure, Steve. See you."

And she would see him—very regularly. That is, until Michelle tired of him. Although Janet herself could not imagine landing such a great guy and then tossing him aside, she had little doubt that Michelle would. After all, for Michelle, there was always a better catch around the corner.

What would it be like, Janet wondered, to have that sort of power? Not that she really wanted it, she assured herself quickly. She tried to imagine herself as a sort of modern-day Helen of Troy, conquering all males within sight—only the image wouldn't come, for Janet was too aware of the heavy sprinkling of freckles on her face and the sturdiness of her frame. With a sigh, she returned to her work. She wondered why she suddenly felt so discontented. By now she should be accustomed to the parade of boys coming to take out Michelle, leaving Janet with books, crafts, and the television set.

But this time it wasn't all Michelle's fault. To be honest, she knew the answer: she was impressed with Steve Wayman.

And someone like Steve could have his choice of girls. When it came to choices, Janet knew she was not even in the running.

Janet tried every excuse in the book and even invented some new ones, but when Saturday came, she found herself on the street corner with her parents watching the parade. To make matters worse, Steve came over and joined them. As

Michelle rode by, her full pink gown spread elegantly across the back of the shiny white convertible, the combined pride of her parents and Steve was just about more than Janet could take. To hear them talk, one would think Michelle was prettier than all the Miss Americas and Miss Universes combined.

Taking a long look at her sister, Janet was aware of the shining dark hair highlighted by the sun, the eager, sincere smile, and the glowing excitement in her deep-blue eyes. Maybe everyone was right, she admitted to herself grudgingly, and the admission caused an ache inside her—an old, familiar ache.

But someday it would be different—someday she would leave Barkley (and Michelle) behind her. However, that was two years away. And two years was an awfully long time.

"See you tonight, Janet," Steve said when the last float had gone by.

"Huh?" she said, slightly confused. "Oh, you mean when you pick up Michelle?"

"Yeah. I'm looking forward to whatever talent you're going to reveal tonight."

"Yes, Steve, I'm sure you are. In fact, I bet that's the main reason you're coming over, isn't it?" Janet winced inwardly as she recognized the sarcastic tone of her own words. She didn't usually reveal her bitterness.

"Hey, hey," Steve said, raising his eyebrows quizzically, "what's this I hear? Shades of green?"

"What's that supposed to mean?" she asked defiantly.

"You wouldn't happen to be jealous of Michelle, would you?"

Janet shook her head at him in disgust. "Forget it, Steve. I have no desire to be Miss Corn Queen and America's Junior Sweetheart. If it sounds like jealousy to you, well . . . just think what you want. You'd never understand the situation. Not in a thousand years."

"Whatever you say, kid," he replied, but his parting grin had a taunting quality. "See you tonight."

Not if I can help it, she thought angrily to herself. This was one night the doorman-butler-receptionist was *not* going to be available. If Mom and Dad were not home, then Steve could ring that doorbell until the end of the world—or until Miss Sloan County opened the door herself—whichever came first.

It was during dinner that Janet put her plan into action.

"Dad, you suppose I could use one of the cars for a while tonight? I won't be out late."

"I don't know why not. Your mother and I were going to take in a movie, but we certainly won't need both cars. If you take mine, though, be prepared to stop for gas. The tank's just about empty. What are your plans, by the way?"

Janet gave him a rather blank look. She really wasn't sure; the only plan was to get out of the house before Steve arrived. She was tired of entertaining guys until Michelle finally decided her date had waited long enough to appreciate her. Janet knew that it would be even worse with Steve.

"I don't mind if you go somewhere," her father said gently, mistaking Janet's blank look for resentment. "It's just that I think we should have some idea where you are."

"Oh," she said, giving him an impish grin. "You mean like that ad on TV: 'Do you know where your children are?' "

"Yes, dear," her mother put in. "For instance, we know Michelle and Steve are going to the skating rink, then for a pizza afterward. No one means to invade your privacy—it just makes good sense. Emergencies can occur, you know."

"Hey, look, I don't mind telling you. It's certainly no secret." Her agile mind flashed to a sign she remembered from the shopping center the last time she had been there. "There's a new arts and crafts supply shop that just opened this week at the shopping center and most of the stores there are open till nine. I just wanted to look over what they had—so I won't be out long."

"Actually, you really should get out more, Janet," her mother said. "Why don't you call Kay or Melissa and do something with them?"

"Like what?"

"Bowling," Nancy suggested. "You could go bowling. Maybe join a league. The pool is open at night or you could go to a movie or out to eat. Or a bunch of you could just cruise the town. Don't kids still go cruising—stopping here and there to talk to other kids and drink a Coke?"

"Yeah, Mom. They still cruise. Don't worry, you're not that much of an antique. Only it's a bit late to make plans now. Besides, Kay and Melissa have dates. So it's okay if I just go to the craft shop? After all, it's what I want to do."

"Who does Kay go with?" Nancy asked. The question was carefully casual, but Janet was sensitive to the hidden meaning: If fat Kay has a boyfriend, why don't you?

"Ronnie Goddard. He's a wimp."

"You could go to the movies with us," Roger suggested. "We'd be glad to have your company."

"Uh, thanks, Dad, but I don't feel like a movie tonight."

From experience, Janet knew that whatever movie her parents had planned to see would be changed to something with a G rating if she went along. And there weren't many of those around. Her father never tried to censor what his daughters saw on their own with friends, but he seemed to suffer excruciating embarrassment at even PG-rated films when his daughters were with him.

The more suggestions her family made, the worse Janet felt. No one would believe she honestly did not mind spending most Friday and Saturday nights alone. What she did mind was the pity she sensed in the air.

Janet might not be one of the popular crowd, but she had

always had plenty of friends—and her two best ones were Kay Freidrich and Melissa Connell. And she really liked them, hoped they would always be her friends. But they both had dates—it was, after all, Saturday night. No doubt there were other high school kids in Barkley who did not have dates. Janet was just not desperate enough to make a point of hunting them up. It wasn't necessary to be social *all* the time, was it? Couldn't a person just be alone occasionally?

Then Michelle decided to add her bit to the conversation. "What happened to Mark Spencer? Remember, you went out with him a few times last year? And there was Johnny Cantrell. He's really quite cute—short but cute."

Janet gritted her teeth at her sister's comments. No one could be that naive. Michelle surely had some idea what had happened with both those guys—as if once were not enough for one lifetime.

Well, she'll never know how I feel, she thought defensively. "They were so juvenile," she said loftily. "*All* the guys in Barkley are just *too* juvenile. I simply am not interested. What's this campaign tonight, anyway, for Pete's sake? I'm fine the way I am."

As quickly as possible, Janet excused herself from the table. Though she couldn't hear it, she knew how the conversation would go after she left the room. "Poor homely Janet," they would say, "I feel so sorry for her. She's such a dud. But you'd think at least one boy would ask her out."

Maybe they would not come right out and say those things, even to each other. But that's exactly what it all boiled down to. She threw herself across her bed and beat her fists into the pillows in frustration. It wasn't fair. It just wasn't fair.

Michelle's careless words had brought those memories of the last school year back to the surface of her mind—memories she had persistently tried to forget. And now they all came back.

Head held down and red-faced, Mark Spencer had asked

her out. Janet had been flattered. She was only a sophomore and he was a senior—a fairly popular one at that. And football homecoming was only a few weeks off. She'd been so pleased and happy. They had gone skating on their first date. The next weekend, they had gone to a movie and Chinese restaurant. Janet admitted to herself that she did not really *like* Mark—she noted a tendency in him to brag and to make jokes at the expense of others. Still, she was determined to go out as long as he asked her. Being with a popular senior was enough—after all, she wasn't expecting to really fall in love yet.

Then Mark began dropping by the house at odd times—completely unannounced. After that, there were no more official dates. He would just hang around the house, only occasionally taking her out briefly for a Coke. Homecoming time grew nearer and Mark had made no mention of it; then he dropped the bombshell.

"Uh, Janet, could you do me a big favor?"

She recalled the feeling of coldness that had stolen over her. It was as if, in the back of her mind, she had known all along.

"What's that, Mark?" she had asked without enthusiasm.

"Well, you see . . . I think of you as a really neat girl—a really good friend . . ."

"Yes?"

"And, well . . . you know, I heard that Michelle and Dennis are breaking up. And I notice he hasn't been here lately. So I was just wondering if—if you'd kind of hint around to her and see if she'd consider going to homecoming with me? You know, just maybe ask her what she thinks of me and see what reaction you get?"

Temper flared inside Janet's head and exploded like a firecracker. "Like heck I will, Mark Spencer! What are you—the gutless wonder? If you can't ask her yourself, you'll never know."

"Hey, listen, redhead, I didn't mean to make you mad."

"My hair isn't red, you double-barreled dipstick. And you didn't make me mad. No one as . . . as unimportant and stupid as you could ever make me mad. You're not worth it. But the fact remains, if you want to date my sister, you'll have to do it on your own."

The hurt had been a long time passing. She knew he hadn't asked her out and *then* gotten interested in Michelle—getting a date with Michelle had been his intention from the beginning. He did not even try to apologize or smooth it over. Not that it would have made any difference.

She really hadn't cared for Mark as a person. It was the idea of being used that hurt.

So why had she let it happen again? Stupidity was the only answer—out-and-out stupidity.

Several weeks later Johnny Cantrell had asked her to be his partner at the ice-skating party held by the science club. Michelle wasn't even going, so Janet told herself Johnny's invitation must be on the level. The worst part of it was that she had actually *liked* him. Certainly she had not suspected he was capable of such cruelty. Then, a few days before their third date was to take place, Janet had overheard a bunch of boys talking in the hall at school.

"You takin' out Janet Lindquist again, John?"

"Yep. Friday night after the game."

"Game's the right word," one boy had taunted. "I know *your* game, Cantrell. Not that I blame you. I'd take Janet out, too, if it gave me a chance to be around Michelle—maybe make a play for her. Now, that is one fox. Great personality, too."

Clutching her books tightly against her, she had waited for Johnny's denial—a denial that had not come. Instead, he had given a short laugh, and said, "Well, after all, all's fair in love and war."

Janet had ducked into a classroom, giving the boys plenty of time to clear out before she emerged. After school, she had located Johnny, looked him right in the eye, and said, "About Friday night, Johnny—something's come up and I won't be able to make it."

He had understood all right. His face had turned a brilliant red. "Janet," he had begun, reaching out to place a restraining hand on her arm. But she had kept on walking away. He had nothing to say that she wanted to hear.

The next day he had passed her a note in geometry class. She thought about throwing it away unread. However, curiosity won out. The note read:

> Janet,
> I know what you must think of me. But your wrong. When the guys kidded me, I just pertended to be cool. I still want to keep our date.
>
> Johnny

Making sure that he could see, she tore the note into little pieces and dropped them on the floor. She did not even bother to look back at him. Who wanted to date a guy who not only couldn't spell, but didn't know a contraction from a possessive? And he hadn't asked again. If he had really wanted to date her, he would have asked again, wouldn't he? From that moment, she had been determined not to be conned a third time.

"Hi, Janet, what have you been doin' this summer? Haven't seen you around much."

Janet turned away from her perusal of the shelves in the new craft store to find Randy Gallagher watching her. He had been a classmate of hers since kindergarten.

"Oh, hi, Randy. I've just been around—no big deal. What about you?"

"I have a summer job. It's just pumpin' gas, but the money's not too bad."

"Great. All I do is baby-sit now and then—not much money there."

"Yeah, well . . . uh, ready for school to start?"

"Not really. But I suppose it doesn't matter. The sooner it starts, the sooner it gets over with."

"Oh, I dunno. School's not so bad in a lot of ways."

Janet shrugged and made no reply, turning her attention back to the paints and brushes. Even though she could not see Randy, she sensed that he was still standing there.

"Uh, Janet, what kind of artwork do you do?"

"I dabble in a little of about everything, but I'm no expert in any of it. What about you?"

"Oils," he said. There was a trace of obvious pride in his announcement. "I just stick with the one thing. Landscapes, portraits, still lifes . . . but all in oils."

"Oh, that's right—I remember now. You took some prizes at the art fair last year."

"Yep. You ever display any of your stuff?"

"Naa. I don't take art in school. It's just a hobby."

"If you'd like to get into oils, I'd be glad to show you some stuff sometime."

"I don't think I'd care to get into oils, Randy. It sounds messy."

He looked puzzled for a moment, then gave a small laugh. "Oh, I get it. I'm slow on the uptake today."

"Today is different?" Janet asked.

"Okay, smart aleck. Just don't say I didn't give you a chance."

"Sure, Randy—I'll remember. How could I forget? You're a real slick operator—in oils."

Randy shook his head and wandered off through the store. While he had been talking to her, Janet had had the feeling he'd wanted something. Perhaps he had been going to ask her out. That could have been what he'd meant about showing her about oil painting. Well, no thanks. She had had enough of that sort of thing.

She could just imagine how it would be: he would suggest all the "lessons" be at her house; then he would roll his big, brown eyes every time Michelle happened to walk through the room—or act depressed if she wasn't around. Randy was nice enough for a friend, but she wasn't about to overstep that boundary and accept a date or an offer of a "demonstration." For as long as she remained in Barkley, she'd just stay dateless. Once she left . . . well, that would be a different story. Then she could be absolutely certain that a guy liked her—not Michelle. Until then, she was taking no more chances. And it didn't matter, anyway. None of the Barkley guys were worth her time, not even Steve Wayman. He wasn't anything special, she told herself, just another of Michelle's admirers.

So why did he keep popping up in her mind?

Chapter Three

Janet was officially a junior. Michelle and Steve were both seniors and still very much together. Of course, Janet had not really expected Michelle to drop him before school started. He was too much of a prize. There was no way Michelle could resist the urge to show she had been the first girl in town to date the gorgeous new guy. In fact, since Steve had proved himself to be a very good running back and was a first-string starter, Janet suspected the romance might last all football season, certainly through football homecoming.

One crisp, autumn Saturday Janet and Kay Freidrich were jogging when they ran into two classmates—Jim Case and Craig Purcell.

"Hey, look at the great athletes," Jim teased. "Getting the old bods in shape?"

"One can always hope," Janet quipped, "although I gotta admit, the prognosis looks pretty glum."

"You said it, kid—we didn't."

"Ah, well, the truth is obvious to all. However, the truth is that I'm thinking of going out for track this spring, so I better get in shape."

Jim eyed her short legs and grinned. "Bet you're no sprinter."

"Nope, but I've got endurance."

"What about you, Kay?" Craig asked. "You going out for shot put?"

Kay glared at him angrily. "Just watch the fat jokes, Craig, or I'll do a little discus practicing with your puny body."

"Hey, who said anything about fat?" he protested, opening his eyes wide in mock innocence. "Jim, did you hear me mention fat?"

"No way, buddy. Guess the poor girl must be paranoid."

"You girls want some practice?" Craig asked. "We'll challenge you to a race—all the way around the school track twice."

Sometime later, the four exhausted teenagers collapsed on a grassy hill near the track.

"You're pretty good, Janet," Jim admitted. "For a girl, that is."

"Am I supposed to thank you for a comment like that?"

"Only if you want to," he replied with a good-natured grin.

Janet pushed her damp hair back off her forehead. It definitely needed cutting; Janet preferred to keep it quite short for easy manageability. With the damp heat, she could feel the curls kinking up tighter. Dislike of her hair was one thing Janet admitted openly, often stating she'd pay a fortune for decent hair—smooth, shining hair with plenty of body without one curl.

"Hey, Janet, by the way, are you going to football homecoming?"

"The game, maybe—not the dance," she answered warily, not looking up.

"Why not?" Jim wanted to know.

"Because I don't want to, dipstick—that's why. Those silly dances do not interest me. Besides, there's not a boy in

Barkley I'd go to a dog fight with."

"Ah, come on," he protested. "We're not that bad."

"That's your opinion."

"Janet Lindquist, you're a real smart aleck."

"Listen, Jim," she said quietly, "you joined us, remember? If you don't like my company, then leave."

"Geez. What a grouch. I like you, Janet, but you're weird. Don't you agree, Craig?"

"Without a doubt. Probably could win the trophy."

Janet grabbed a handful of grass and stuffed it down Jim's sweat shirt. He was quick to retaliate and soon all four were wrestling about, pulling up grass and throwing it at each other.

"I surrender!" Kay finally cried. "Let's just forget it—I'm probably going to get hives from this grass now."

"If you get 'em all over," Jim cracked, "it's gonna be bad, 'cause you sure have a lot to cover."

Kay just shook her head complacently. Ever since she had been going with Ronnie, the jokes about her weight did not seem to upset her as they once had. Janet surmised that the few dates had given her confidence and she no longer had to be so defensive. *And* she was doing something about it at last: she was dieting and exercising and the pounds were slowly coming off.

"Come on," Craig suggested, "let's go on up to the machines and get a soda."

After they had had their drinks and relaxed a while longer, the boys took off.

"Ready to jog home?" Janet asked Kay.

"Yep. Just let me tie my shoe."

While she was bent down over the shoe, she began talking. "You know, Janet, I think Jim was trying to ask you to the homecoming dance."

"Then why didn't he?" she asked nonchalantly. "I was here, wasn't I?"

"You know very well why he didn't. You kept mouthing

off—didn't give him a chance. It isn't easy for most boys to ask a girl out, you know."

"Listen to the expert," Janet joked. To tell the truth, Kay could be really irritating sometimes. She went out with one guy a few times and suddenly felt qualified to offer advice.

"I know I'm no expert," her friend replied mildly, "but I'm right about this. He meant to ask you and you scared him off."

"He wasn't mad at what I said," Janet argued. "We were just kidding around."

"Yeah, sure. I know he didn't get mad, but he didn't ask you out, either. He wasn't sure if you meant what you said."

"I did mean what I said, Kay. Only not in a mean way. Jim's all right—so's Craig. For friends, that is. I'm just not interested in dating them. Not going to the dance doesn't bother me in the least. Now, are you ready to jog home?"

"Ready as I'll ever be. Only I can't figure you out, Janet. I really can't."

"Then don't try. Just run."

Some people confided in their friends, Janet thought as she ran. But she just couldn't open up and do that. It would all sound like jealousy, but the problem was deeper than that and she doubted that she could make Kay or anyone else understand just how hard it was to be Michelle Lindquist's sister.

"Hey, Janet, where've you been hiding?"

Recognizing Steve's voice without looking up, Janet continued to scrub the lawn chairs. What a crummy job to be stuck with! Mom had told her to clean up all the outdoor furniture and put it away in the basement. This was a warm, sunny Saturday, but it would not be long before winter made itself felt, and Janet's mother did not believe in procrastinating.

"Who's hiding? I'm usually around someplace."

"Seems to me it's been a long time since I saw you."

And that's the way I want it, Janet said to herself. No more free predate shows. The memory was still with her of Steve's easy laughter the evening she had juggled and tap-danced for him.

"Whatcha doin'?" he asked.

Janet just rolled her eyes in disgust at Steve's dumb question. She turned the hose on the chair to rinse off the soap from the Brillo pad.

"I'm gathering daisies, Stephen."

"That's what I thought. May I help?"

"If you want."

He picked up an extra pad and began scrubbing the wrought-iron bench. "Daisies were always my favorite. Be good and I'll pick some extras and make a wreath for your head. Daisies will look great in your red hair."

"My hair isn't red," she said indignantly. "It's strawberry-blond."

"Whatever you say," he agreed with a wide grin. "Only, it seems to me that it's a lot more strawberry than blond."

Janet deftly adjusted the nozzle on the hose to spray and turned it in Steve's direction.

"Hey, cut it out!" he protested.

"Take it back," she demanded, "or I turn it on full force."

"I take it back, Janet. You're the blondest person I know."

"That's better. Much better."

Careless of the wet grass, he sat down on the ground and scrubbed the legs of the bench.

"You don't have to do that, you know, Steve."

"I know I don't. But who wouldn't want to gather daisies? It's one of my favorite things."

"I see. Do the guys on the football team know that?"

"Sure. What does it matter? After all, Rosie Grier does needlepoint and nobody's going to take him on."

"Well, I don't care much for this daisy picking. So if that's the way you get your jollies, go to it. Glad for the help."

"Speaking of football," he said, "you don't go to the games much, do you?"

"Oh . . . once in a while. Not all the time."

"Why not? Don't you have any school spirit?"

She really didn't, but it sounded awful just to say so. The fact was, Janet did not go to the games much because of the cheerleaders. Michelle was one and it always made her feel funny, as though people were looking at *her*, staring at her in the stands and comparing her unfavorably to the pretty girl out in front with the short skirt and pom-poms.

"I dunno, Steve," she finally said. "I'm always glad when they win, of course. I guess I just usually have other things to do."

"Like what? Enamel lids and more daisy picking?"

"Why not?"

"So skip those marvelous activities this Friday night. Come watch me play."

"Just you? Not the whole team?" she cracked.

"After all, I'm the best part," he kidded. "And it's our homecoming game—and a conference game. We need all the support we can get. Will you?"

"I'll think about it."

"Please do—for me."

Although she did not say a word, Janet felt a familiar bitterness sweep over her. What earthly difference could it make to Steve Wayman if she were at the game or not? His eyes would be on *his* girl—on Michelle. What little time he had to look, that is. Michelle was the one he was taking to the dance afterward.

Michelle's new deep-blue velvet pants suit had been hemmed and was in her closet, ready to wear. Steve would come to the house, all dressed up in his suit, awkwardly carrying a florist's box, and would try to pin the corsage trimmed with a tiny gold football on the lapel of Michelle's blazer. Janet could see it all now. And if she was home, she could sit in the corner and watch. No thanks.

"Is something wrong?" Steve asked gently.

"No, of course not. Why?"

"Your eyes had a faraway look—and you have a terrible scowl on your face."

Janet shrugged. "I guess all this daisy picking is getting to me." She wearily wiped her arm across her face.

"Now you've got pink soap on your nose," he told her.

"Good thing my hair isn't red, then. Pink and red don't match at all. And I want to look nice while I'm daisy picking."

Steve rose solemnly and placed an imaginary crown on Janet's head. "Now you do look nice. The daisies look great on your hair—whatever color you call it. You'd look awfully pretty if you'd just get that scowl off your face."

His fingertips brushed her cheek and he looked deeply into her eyes, trying to coax a smile from her.

Smile? She felt more like crying. Here she stood with wet jeans, soap drying on her nose, and her nearly red hair a mass of tangles. And he said she was pretty. Am I supposed to be grateful for his crumbs? she thought. She was bewildered by the feelings she had when Steve looked at her that way and touched her face. This was Michelle's boyfriend, so what was she doing going all mushy over him? There was no way she was going to permit that.

"Hey," he said loudly, "now you're frowning even more. Don't you like the wreath I placed upon your head, my Princess Daisy?"

Janet had to fight down the urge to say, Go place it on Michelle's head, because she knew Steve would take such a comment as jealousy. He had already accused her of that once. If he wanted her to smile, she'd smile.

"I like it fine, Steve. It fits just right." She smiled at him then, letting the dimples appear in her cheeks.

"That's much better."

"Great, now *you* bend over."

"What for?"

" 'Cause I've made a crown for you, too. And I can't reach your tall head."

Obligingly, Steve bent slightly and Janet gravely placed a used-up Brillo pad on his crown.

"It's only one daisy," she apologized mockingly, "but it's encased in gold—very masculine."

"And how do I look?"

"Like a king for sure."

He took her hand and, holding it up in the air, led her toward the still wet bench and motioned for her to sit down. He then sat beside her. "Just like royalty," he announced.

"I think royalty is getting wet in the rear from this bench."

"It doesn't matter," he said severely. "That's part of being monarchs—holding down the throne despite damp, dew, blight, and locusts."

"I suppose you're right. But it's all such a chore, especially when those locusts fly up your nose."

"Janet, are you working or playing?" Nancy called from the back deck.

"A little of both," she yelled back honestly. "I'm almost done—just have to take it to the basement."

"I'll help," Steve volunteered.

"Gosh, why are you being so nice today? Want something?"

"Janet, I'm hurt. Here I'm just being my normal, sweet self and get accused of ulterior motives."

"I'm sorry, Your Royal Hindness."

"Hindness? Boy, I get no respect."

"Maybe you don't deserve any respect. With me, you gotta earn it. I don't just give respect to any old king."

"If giving you a crown, having you share my throne, and helping lug this junk around doesn't earn it, what will? You're a hard woman, Janet."

"Yep," she agreed. "Treat 'em rough—that's my motto."

"I believe it," he said, giving a groan as he picked up the heavy bench.

"And my mother expected me to carry this stuff all by myself. No wonder I'm a hard woman—it's an inherited characteristic."

Steve laughed as much as his load would allow him to. "Ah, Janet, you're always good for a laugh."

"Thanks," she said dryly.

"Hey, kiddo, that's a compliment. You're great company—I like being around you."

Janet swallowed hard, not knowing what to say. She wanted to make another wisecrack but, for once, none popped into her head.

When the lawn furniture was all stashed away in the basement, Janet turned her attention to putting away the hose and cleaning supplies. Steve cheerfully helped coil the hose.

"Well, thanks a lot for helping," she said somewhat awkwardly.

"Don't mention it. I'm always glad for the opportunity to help a pretty girl gather daisies."

She watched in silence as he crossed from her yard to his own in a few easy strides. Steve Wayman was quite a fellow. So different from all the normal, run-of-the-mill Barkley nerds. Why did he have to move here, anyway? It would have been so much simpler if he had never come here in the first place.

Until she walked out the door and climbed in the car, Janet had not been certain she was going to the football game. Even now, as she moved the car down the familiar Barkley streets, she didn't know exactly why she was going.

Once there, she had a good time. She sat down on the bleachers among her friends, got caught up in the excitement of the game, and yelled along with the others until she was hoarse.

The half-time festivities weren't even too bad. Emily was homecoming queen; for once, Michelle hadn't won. Janet knew she should feel little and mean because she was glad Michelle hadn't won. However, she didn't—she merely felt a twinge of satisfied relief.

When the game was over—Barkley won by a last-minute field goal—Janet got down from the bleachers and started walking toward the student parking lot. Her car was near the gym, and through the window she caught sight of the bright decorations. The school colors of gold and white blended nicely with the mums and multicolored leaves. Gold, white, and brown crepe paper strands were looped across the ceiling and down the walls. It caused her to feel an undeniable ache deep inside. And she was puzzled by the ache. After all, she didn't care about the silly dance.

Well, one thing she wasn't going to do was head straight home. The kids who were going to the dance were hurrying home to change clothes. Janet had no desire to watch her parents take pictures of Michelle and Steve before the dance.

"Hey, Janet," someone called, "wait up."

Janet snapped out of her unpleasant reverie to see Melissa running toward her. "Wanta cruise around town for a while—maybe get something to eat somewhere? I'm starved."

"You're not going to the dance?" Janet was mystified. It was all Kay and Melissa had talked about all week long.

"Wouldn't you know?" Melissa said with a philosophical shrug. "Phil has mono. His folks made him go to the doctor today because he's been so tired lately. Now he has to stay in bed for a while. He tried to get me to go without him—said he'd ask one of his buddies who didn't have a date to take me. But I told him it was no big deal. I'd rather not go if I couldn't go with him."

"Well, then, sure—let's go. Only I guess I better call my folks from somewhere and let them know I won't be home for a while."

Janet was surprised at the relief that was flooding over her. She had not looked forward to riding around alone just to kill time until she was sure Michelle and Steve had had time to clear out.

To Janet's dismay, she saw Steve's Camaro pull up in front of the house just after she had parked the station wagon in the carport. Here she had managed to avoid the Beautiful Pair, as she sometimes thought of them, before the dance—only to run into them afterward.

Cautiously, she opened the car door hoping to sneak into the house unnoticed. She was somewhat surprised then to see Michelle suddenly spring from the passenger side of the car and run toward the house alone. Steve made no move to get out of the car and follow. Lover's quarrel, Janet thought cynically, and she got out of the car.

"Janet?"

Fighting an urge to run into the house, Janet turned around.

"What do you want, Steve?"

"Can I talk to you a minute?"

"Yeah, I guess so."

She walked toward him, hoping he wouldn't tell her his problems. If Steve and Michelle had had trouble, she did not want to get involved. She did not want to be asked to help patch things up.

"Didn't see you at first," he said. "Then when the interior lights of your car came on, I saw your not red hair shining like a beacon."

"How poetic."

"Just another of my talents," he said.

"Yeah? Well, I don't think Robert Frost has anything to worry about."

"Hey, I might surprise you someday. Saw you at the game. Thanks for coming."

"You actually saw me? I thought you were supposed to be playing."

"Well, after all, I don't play every single second. There are time-outs and half-time, you know. Besides, I'm so good I can watch the girls and carry the ball simultaneously."

"Your modesty overwhelms me."

He shrugged and grinned, but Janet noticed that the grin did not extend to his eyes. Even from the dim light of the street lamp, she could tell that.

"It was a good game," she said lamely, hoping to keep him off the subject, hoping to keep him from telling her Michelle had broken his heart.

The tactic did not work.

"Michelle and I broke up tonight."

"Well, don't feel too bad, Steve. You lasted longer than most of them." She thought to herself that she had guessed right. Michelle had held on till after football homecoming. This gave her plenty of time to find another guy before the round of Christmas parties.

"She says she wants to date other guys. Namely Jordan McNeill."

Janet nodded her head in quick understanding. Jordan was in his third year of college, but he'd be home soon for the long semester break—just in time for all the holiday festivities.

"Then I guess you can date other girls, Steve," she said unsympathetically.

"Yep, I suppose so. Only I'm not sure I want to."

"You're *that* hung up on Michelle?" Janet asked, feeling bitter that she had gotten trapped into listening to all this.

"Oh, I don't know. Sure, she's a hard act to follow . . ."

You're telling me! Janet thought angrily.

"Besides," he continued, "there's not much future in dating in high school."

Janet laughed at that one. "Come on, Steve. Does there have to be a future in it? I thought it was just a pastime—something to do for fun."

"*You* don't date," he pointed out. "You must not think there's any future there, either."

"Did it ever occur to you that maybe I wasn't asked out?"

"Nope. Michelle told me you used to date, then just stopped. And Jim Case told me he was going to ask you out and you gave him some putdown before he had the chance. So I figure it's all your choice—you'd rather work on your enamel boxes."

"And pick daisies," she added lightly, hoping to keep him from guessing the truth behind her dateless life-style.

Steve glanced at his watch. "You want to go for a hamburger or something? It's not late yet."

"I'm not really hungry. Melissa and I pigged out just a little bit ago."

"Then you could keep me company while *I* pig out. I'm always starved after a game."

"Look, Steve, I'll level with you. I'm just in no mood to have my shoulder cried on. So it's a new experience for you—it's an old one for me. Michelle dumps guys all the time. She's my sister and I love her, but that's just the simple truth. And who can say what's right? Maybe she *is* right. Getting serious when you're still in high school is for the birds."

Steve gave her an odd look.

"I'm not going to cry, Janet. And I wasn't serious about Michelle—not the way you make it sound. I guess it's all a matter of pride. She's just about the prettiest and most popular girl in the whole school, so it made me feel really great to be seen with her. And I admit I'd rather dump than be dumped, not that either situation is pleasant. So come with me or stay here—it's up to you."

"It's not a date, is it?" she asked cautiously. "Because I make it a policy not to date Michelle's rejects on the rebound."

Steve laughed and shook his head. "Janet, you are really good for a person's ego, the tactful way you put things. This 'reject' is just asking a friend to go for a bite to eat. As I said, take it or leave it."

And standing there in the front of the house, Janet faced a fact: she wanted to go. It was dumb and illogical, but she wanted to go. And what could it hurt? This time she knew from the beginning that it was no date, that it was Michelle he was interested in. So there could be no misunderstanding.

"Well, okay," she said slowly.

"Don't appear so eager," he teased.

"What do you want me to do? Melt like butter, cling to your arm, and say, 'Oh, Steve, how wonderful of you to ask me'?"

"Try it," he said with a grin. "You might like it."

"Thanks, but no thanks. I'll just tell my folks I'm going out again."

In just a few seconds, Janet was settled in the bucket seat. She looked over at Steve's strong profile and felt suddenly shy. Only it wasn't a date, she told herself. Not a date at all—so she'd just have to keep him laughing.

"Hey, Steve?"

"Hmmmm?"

"How many football players does it take to change a light bulb?"

"Don't start with the football jokes," Steve warned, laughing.

"Okay, if you're going to be picky, how about this one? Why did the elephant paint his toenails red?"

And to a barrage of silly prattle, the Camaro moved on down the street.

Janet, the not redheaded girl, found that she enjoyed her not-date very much. Too much.

Only he wasn't going to know that. Not if she could help it.

Chapter Four

"Janet, are you going to make me one of these things for Christmas?"

"Oh, I don't know," she replied somewhat crossly. "If you really want to help with this, then hold the silly thing still. I can't sand it properly if you wiggle it all over the place."

"Then let me do the sanding. You can do the artistic work. Now, hand over the sandpaper."

Janet gave a deep sigh, and surrendered the piece of sandpaper and the wooden box to Steve. This had never been her favorite part of the project, anyway.

"Well, are you?" he repeated.

"Am I what?"

"Going to make me one for Christmas."

"What would you do with one? They aren't exactly masculine, you know."

"Who says they're not? You made your dad one, didn't you?"

"Yeah, but that's different. He has a desk so he can use it to hold little stuff."

"I have a desk," Steve announced with a comically important air.

"You have a desk? What on earth for? I've never seen it."

"Come over to my house sometime and see for yourself," he told her with a grin. "It's in my room. It's for doing homework and taking care of other important business matters."

"Great. Have any arisen yet?"

"A few."

"Very few, I would imagine."

"Janet, you just fail to understand me. You're always underestimating me. People bring matters of grave importance to me for help. I suppose you're always in such a dream world that you can't even see what's taking place next door to your own home."

"Me in a dream world? Nonsense. I'm the most practical person I know."

"Then why all the unicorns?"

"What do unicorns have to do with practicality?"

"Nothing at all. Unicorns have to do with fantasy. See, I caught you in your own trap."

"Steve, why are you suddenly harping on unicorns?"

"Because you paint them over and over. You use designs with unicorns in them far more than you do anything else. And unicorns aren't even real. Therefore, I surmise that you are retreating into fantasy."

"Give up on amateur psychology, Steve. I do like unicorns, but I seriously doubt that there is any deep meaning behind it."

"That's because you don't know about such things," he said smugly.

Janet flipped one of her dad's shop towels at him.

"Hey," he protested. "You'll make me drop this thing—and after all the time I've spent on it, I don't want it dented."

"You can't dent wood, dummy."

"Why not?"

"You just can't."

"You can so dent wood."

"You two sound like a pair of four-year-olds," Michelle said as she sauntered through the room.

"So who asked your opinion?" Janet mumbled, but the mumble was loud enough for Michelle to hear.

Without really looking up, Janet was fully aware of her sister's appearance—hair caught back on one side with a fancy barrette, new tight designer jeans, and a sweater that must have cost a month's allowance. She glared down at her own sawdust-covered baggy corduroys and glumly rubbed her grimy hands across her knees. Now that Michelle had appeared, there was a subtle but unmistakable change in the atmosphere. Everybody was trying not to look at everybody else—that's what the real problem was.

It had been that way the past few weeks, ever since Michelle and Steve had broken up. Although they had never discussed it, Janet knew exactly why Steve was around so much—and what he was hoping for. He wanted to be around when Michelle decided she had had enough of Jordan. And it didn't really bother Janet. After all, she was in on it from the beginning this time.

"Consider it a gift," Michelle said airily with a charming smile.

"What did you say?" Janet had even forgotten she had said anything.

"You wanted to know who asked for my opinion," Michelle reminded her.

"Oh, I see. Most kind of you."

"Think nothing of it."

"How astute of you, Michelle. Nothing is exactly what I think of it."

Michelle shook her head in exaggerated dismay. "Did you ever know a bigger smart aleck than my sister, Steve?"

"Well, let's say that I've never known a worse one—but I wouldn't call her big. What are you, anyway, Janet, about four feet ten?"

Janet took note of the fact that Steve managed to answer

Michelle without ever looking directly at her.

"Listen, let's watch the size remarks. I happen to be five feet two inches."

Steve grinned at her. "Uh-huh, and I'm the jolly green giant."

"I am so five two."

"There you two go again, arguing like infants," Michelle said. "Well, if you'll excuse me, I'm going out for a bit."

"You're excused," Janet said shortly. "And take as long as you like."

Michelle gave a deep sigh and left without bothering to answer.

"Really, Janet," Steve said with mock solemnity. Janet was very aware that he had made a distinct point of not turning around and looking at Michelle as she left—had not even said good-bye. Probably because he could not bear to, she supposed.

"Really, what?"

"When are you ever going to see yourself as you really are?"

"I do see myself as I really am. And what's that comment supposed to mean, anyway?"

"When I look at you, I see a short, red-haired girl who lives in a dream world. But you think you're a tall, practical strawberry-blonde."

Janet gave a short laugh. "Well, Steve, I guess we can't both be right."

"And surely *I* can't be wrong," he taunted.

"Maybe I just don't like what I am."

"Why not? I like what you are."

"Really, Steve, do you?" A tinge of bitterness made itself felt in the words. This was the closest she and Steve had come to a serious conversation and she was finding it an uncomfortable experience.

"Listen, Janet. It takes all kinds to make a world. We need short, redheaded dreamers. There's nothing wrong with unicorns."

Janet ran her finger over the enameled top of one of her completed boxes on a nearby table. "But like you said a while ago, unicorns aren't real."

"Maybe they can be if you want them to badly enough," he said softly.

"So now who's being impractical?"

"We all have our moments, Janet."

After that, they returned to working on the boxes in a companionable silence broken only by an occasional silly comment. Maybe Steve did like her, she thought—as a friend. She should be satisfied with that, she guessed. Yet she knew she really wasn't.

"Steve's sure around here a lot," Michelle said casually at dinner that night.

Janet resisted the urge to fling a forkful of spaghetti in her direction. Michelle knew exactly why Steve Wayman was "around here a lot." She just wanted to rub it in.

"Yes," Nancy replied calmly, "he and Janet seem to really hit it off. Sounds as if they have a good time together."

"If you ask *me,*" Michelle said, "they sound like a pair of little kids. In fact, that's exactly what I told them this afternoon."

"So?" Roger said, lifting one eyebrow. "If that's what they enjoy, who are they hurting?"

"Oh, Dad, I didn't mean they were hurting anyone."

"Okay, Michelle. I just thought maybe you were upset because Steve comes to see Janet instead of you."

Michelle nearly dropped her breadstick. Good old Dad, Janet thought, chuckling to herself. Leave it to him to completely misunderstand a situation. But not for long, she'd wager. There was no way Michelle was going to let her father keep believing Steve had thrown *her* over.

"Really, Father, are you purposely dense? Breaking up with Steve was *my* idea."

"Why?" he asked in disbelief. Roger was honestly incredulous. "Why would anyone willingly break up with a fine young man like Steve?"

"I just like to date a lot of different guys, rather than go with the same one all the time. Isn't that okay?"

"Sure, it's fine with me," he said, though obviously still unclear about the whole thing. "And I guess it's fine with everyone else. As your mother said, Steve and Janet really seem to hit it off."

"It isn't the same thing." Janet heard her own words ring loudly and clearly in the air.

"Pardon?" Nancy asked.

"Steve and I don't go together. We're just friends—that's all."

"Do you really think so?" Nancy asked dubiously. "He's here an awful lot—not that I mind. He's a polite and helpful boy. And he certainly takes you lots of places."

"As a friend," Janet insisted.

"Well, after all, I don't know what else you'd expect, anyway," Nancy continued. "We need to do something about your wardrobe. It isn't that I want to get rid of some money, but we must go shopping and get you some new things. If you looked more like a girl, why, then, Steve would probably 'go with you' instead of just hanging around—or whatever terms you use."

"Oh, Mom. Parents always misunderstand everything. Sometimes I think you do it on purpose. It's the way *I* want it, too, for Pete's sake."

"Hmmmm. Whatever you say. But I still want you to keep Saturday free."

Janet gritted her teeth and maintained silence. With her mother on this kick, she had a pretty good idea what she'd get for Christmas, too: clothes. Instead of a new tennis racket and some really good art supplies, she'd get sweet little dresses and dressy slacks, and frilly blouses. The idea was nauseating. She knew that pretty clothes wouldn't attract Steve. He was still interested in Michelle and there was nothing Janet could do about it.

Christmas was in the air.

Downtown Barkley was fully decorated with bells on every streetlight and bright tinsel in every store window.

Janet didn't have much shopping to do; she had made the boxes for all of her grandparents, cousins, and close friends. Her parents and Michelle, however, were already well supplied with her handiwork and she needed to buy gifts for them.

She found a delicate gold chain for Michelle, a cologne gift set for her mother, and some kind of weird tool her father had been wanting. At a specialty shop, she found some really different gift-wrapping paper and purchased it along with matching ribbon.

Back home, she shut herself up in her room to wrap her gifts. After everything else was wrapped, she turned around slowly and regarded the rectangular-shaped wooden box on her dresser. The white unicorn stood proudly in the middle of exotic foliage—trees bearing fruit and blossoms unlike anything seen in the real world. It was one of her better boxes. It would not be at all out of place on a guy's desk or bureau. And he had kidded her about giving him one, hadn't he? It wasn't like it was a real gift. Neither of them would have to be embarrassed if he didn't have anything for her, which he wouldn't. Why should he? The box was just a silly thing she'd made. If she wanted to give it to Steve—almost as a joke—then why shouldn't she?

Having made up her mind, she carefully placed the wooden box inside a cardboard one and wrapped it up in Santa Claus paper—maybe he'd get a bang out of having his present wrapped in kiddie paper.

"For me? Janet, you shouldn't have."

She felt unaccountably embarrassed and knew her face was turning scarlet.

"It's not much," she muttered, feeling really dumb at saying such a trite thing.

"But here's yours," he announced, grinning impishly and withdrawing a small box from his pocket.

"Oh, Steve—*you* shouldn't have."

"Yeah, I know. But I'm really a great guy."

Janet looked at the small red-and-gold package in her hand. Whatever it was, she'd treasure it always. She knew that without looking—knew it and didn't want to know it.

Steve tore into his with typical male enthusiasm, careless of the wrappings.

"You're tearing Santa's head off," she complained.

"So what do you want me to do? Unwrap it daintily and save it till next year? You think this is the Depression or something?"

"My gosh, Steve, you never know. It could be coming—that's what my grandfathers always say. And that paper you are treating with such disrespect cost a buck a sheet."

When he got down to opening the box itself, Janet felt embarrassed all over again. Giving him a homemade box with a unicorn lid had really been a dumb idea. Why hadn't she just bought him some after-shave or something?

"Hey," he said softly, lifting out the box. "That's really great. I was hoping you'd make me one." And he did look genuinely pleased. Janet wondered if he really was or if he was just a good actor.

"You did a nice job—that unicorn looks like he's ready to jump out at me. King of all he surveys, isn't he?"

"Only he's not real."

"Sure he is. Because I want him to be."

"Is wanting enough to make it real?"

"It is if you want it hard enough. Now, aren't you going to open yours?"

Janet touched the gold bow uneasily. She tried to prepare

herself for a gag gift. After all, that was what her relationship with Steve was—a gag.

Swallowing hard, she lifted the lid from the small box. Inside was a gold locket on a chain. So maybe it was a gag gift, she told herself quickly. Steve surely knew she wasn't the jewelry type. The locket was oval-shaped and, on the front, bore a small, single daisy. Each white petal was delicately and perfectly formed around the yellow center. She looked up at him in surprise.

"Open it," he said with a smile.

Janet carefully opened it up. Instead of the traditional picture of a person, the locket contained a tiny picture of a unicorn. "Ohhh," she said, taking a long breath. "Where did you find something like this?"

"It wasn't easy. I had to enlist Mom's help. That is, in finding the unicorn. I found the locket myself and nothing else would do—I felt you deserved a real daisy. And after we had that conversation about unicorns, I thought the picture would be a neat touch. After all, you're always giving them to other people. Poor Mom had to look high and low for that picture."

"I can imagine. There aren't many of us unicorn fanciers around."

For a moment she was lost for words and a mist threatened to form in her eyes. Stubbornly she blinked back the moisture.

"You're a great pal, Steve," she said.

"Am I, Janet? Are you sure?"

"I don't know what that's supposed to mean," she said glibly. "Don't you want to be my pal, Steve?"

She punched him lightly in the stomach and draped the red ribbon from his package around his neck.

The look he gave her was distinctly odd, but it passed quickly. He shrugged, took the locket from her and fastened it around her neck, and then tousled her hair as if she were a small child.

"Hey, watch it, Steve," she protested. "You're gonna mess up my hairdo."

"That's a hairdo? Looks more like a hairdon't to me."

"Yeah? And what do you think yours looks like?"

"Great, as always."

"You'll look great when I get done with you," she warned, reaching out to pull at his hair.

They wrestled around on the floor, as Michelle had said, like a pair of four-year-olds. They were the best of pals. Janet was relieved that the odd, misty moment had passed. Only a small ache persisted somewhere down deep inside.

"Wear that dark-green dress," Nancy commanded.

"Oh, Mom, do I have to? Can't I just wear slacks? What about those nice brown ones?"

"No, Janet, wear the dress. And don't argue. The Waymans are having a lot of people in for this party and I want you to look nice."

Knowing she had no choice, Janet went off to her room to change, not even trying to be a good sport about it.

The whole thing sounded really dumb to her, anyway. It was Christmas night—the packages were open and everyone was still stuffed from Christmas dinner. What kind of people had a party on Christmas night, for Pete's sake? Obviously Margaret and Bill, she said, answering her own question. "Just a little buffet—light snacks and plenty of good company," Margaret had said. Big deal. Janet would much rather stay home. As she had suspected, most of her packages did contain clothing; but there was one nice set of paints and she was itching to try them out.

She knew her mother had bought the dress for her because it was green, and green should look good on Janet since she almost had red hair. Only *should* didn't necessarily mean it would.

Feeling thoroughly disgruntled, she pulled on the hated panty hose and stepped into her high-heeled shoes. Then she slipped on the green wool dress and fastened the belt. Looking in the mirror, she was not impressed. She combed her hair as quickly as possible and started back into the living room, then hesitated and turned back. Slowly she lifted the locket from its box, fastened it around her neck, and let it rest against the deep-green background of her dress. On impulse, she added a touch of pale, coral-colored lipstick. Perhaps she did not look *too* bad—for her.

Her moment of satisfaction was very brief. It lasted until she saw Michelle all decked out in a frilly white blouse and chic slender skirt. Her heels were much higher than Janet's and she seemed to tower over her—like a model, Janet thought glumly. Pretty, tall, slender, poised.

Steve's eyes lit up when they walked into the room after Bill had taken their coats in the foyer. And Janet couldn't blame him. Everyone reacted that way to Michelle; it was just a fact of life. Even Janet had to admit she looked like something that had just stepped out of a display window on Park Avenue.

Not being able to watch the look of longing on Steve's face—and being cross with herself for not being able to—Janet glanced away from him quickly and moved across the room. The Waymans had certainly gone all out. The house was gorgeously decorated and the buffet table was laden with attractively prepared foods.

"You look so nice tonight," Margaret said, catching Janet by the shoulder and giving her a hug. She sounded slightly surprised at her own observation, Janet thought. While she realized she was not exactly gorgeous, she also knew Margaret was accustomed to seeing her in jeans and sweat shirts.

"Thank you," she said. "Your house looks real great. Gosh, how did you manage it? Ours looks like a rat trap—everyone still has gifts piled all over the place because we don't know where to put them."

"Just don't open any closed doors, Janet, or things are likely to start falling out at you."

"Okay, whatever you say. When do we get to eat? That stuff really looks good."

Margaret laughed. Janet was a bit chagrined. No doubt that was not exactly a gracious, smooth thing to say—not at all what Michelle would have said.

"Oh, soon, dear. When all of the guests have arrived. Your locket looks nice with that dress."

"Yeah, it's really pretty. Thanks for helping Steve with it."

"It was fun, and quite a challenge. Steve enjoys your company so much, Janet."

"Yeah? Well, he's a good friend. We're alike in a lot of ways."

"You are? I hadn't exactly noticed that. I thought it was more a case of opposites attracting."

"There's no attraction involved," Janet said quickly. "We just goof around together."

As soon as she could without seeming impolite, Janet moved out of Margaret's path. No matter what Steve's mother thought, they were alike in a couple of very important areas: they shared a similar sense of humor—and even though Janet went about it more openly, Steve always understood and was able to carry it on; and they were rejects—both suffering because of Michelle. It wasn't anything they talked about, but Janet felt it was certainly their strongest bond.

She wandered around the decorated rooms, feeling lost, until it was announced that refreshments were ready. Janet lost no time in heading for the line and heaping her plate with hot and cold snacks. Moving to a quiet corner of the room, she found an empty ottoman and sat down to eat.

"Hey, where have you been? I saw you when you first came in and then you completely disappeared."

Janet looked up to see Steve towering over her.

She wanted to say, Of course you didn't see me walk off; you were too busy mooning over Michelle. Instead she merely shrugged and dipped a shrimp into some cocktail sauce.

"May I join you?"

"Suit yourself," she said, chewing vigorously.

"Not exactly friendly tonight, are we," he observed with a grin, sitting down on the carpeted floor, crossing his long legs in front of him.

"I'm all right," she mumbled. "Just not used to standing around dressed up like a prize cow."

His grin grew wider. "I don't believe I ever saw a cow in dark-green wool. But I think you look very nice, Janet. Don't you think beauty is worth a little discomfort?"

"Is that how you feel about it?"

Steve pulled at his tie with a rueful smile. "I don't know. I guess it just takes getting used to."

"Hey, look," someone called from across the room. "Steve's got a girl cornered under the mistletoe."

Janet felt her heart stop. Warily she looked up. And it was there all right—green leaves and white berries suspended from the ceiling. She supposed it was someone's idea of fun, a little something to liven up the party. But she could see nothing funny in the situation.

Her face grew redder and redder as people began to call out things like "Pucker up, Steve," and "I'll trade places with you, boy, if you can't handle it."

Steve, however, did not seem in the least embarrassed. He calmly put down his plate, rose to his knees, put one hand at the back of Janet's neck, and kissed her firmly on the lips.

She raised both hands and placed them on his shoulders with every intention of pushing him away. With his face only an inch from hers, he whispered softly, "Just go along with it, kid. It won't kill you to be a good sport. I'm not poison."

No, he wasn't poison, she thought bitterly. He was cute and part of her wanted him to kiss her. Only she knew she couldn't allow that part to rule her. This time, however, she appeared to be trapped. It was just a game, a silly trick, and it meant nothing at all. She swallowed hard, moved her face toward Steve's to close the minute gap, and their lips met again. This time the kiss was soft, but long and lingering. Janet let her lips move beneath his, loving the touch and taste of him.

When he pulled back at last, there was applause from the onlookers and Janet felt herself flush once more.

The look Steve was giving her was different from the ones she had seen before, almost . . . well, almost tender. Perhaps he guessed that she was beginning to fall for him and felt sorry for her.

It could grow to be a bad situation—Steve pining after Michelle and Janet pining after Steve.

She pushed back all these thoughts, looked out into the crowd of smiling faces, and said loudly, "Well, it wasn't too bad. But I think I prefer the shrimp cocktail, so clear the way to the table."

It brought a big laugh and Steve laughed right along with the others, but a flicker of emotion she could not define moved across his eyes and was quickly gone. He followed her to the buffet table.

"I could have sworn you enjoyed that," he joked.

She shrugged indifferently. "Our relationship is purely platonic, Steve."

"Yeah, I guess I forgot." He didn't sound too happy, but he loaded his plate once more and was able to eat it all. The touchy subject did not come up again and Janet skillfully managed to avoid any more mistletoe.

When she went to bed that night, she thought about wearing the locket but was afraid she would break the chain. She put it away in its little box very carefully and, when the lights were out, all she could think about was Steve Wayman. Over and over again she felt his hand on her neck and his gentle kiss.

Against her will, hot tears began to roll down her cheeks. Though she'd tried not to, she had fallen in love with Steve. And that made her a fool, an utter and complete fool.

Maybe she had to be honest with herself and admit it, but she could keep Steve—and everyone else—from knowing. Because she didn't want anyone's pity.

Janet Lindquist was independent and a free soul. And she was going to make certain everyone saw her that way.

Chapter Five

"You gonna tell me why you keep enameling box lids?" Steve asked. He roamed restlessly about the Lindquist living room while she worked.

"Why not?" she countered without even looking up.

"What are you going to do with them? It's a whole year till next Christmas. Besides, you've already given everyone you know one of those things."

"Those 'things,' " Janet said indignantly. "What a way to refer to my works of art. If you have no more appreciation than that, I'll take your unicorn box back. You'd get just as much use and pleasure out of a cigar box."

"Don't go knocking cigar boxes. They're great. When I was a kid, I used to collect them. It got started when my grandfather gave me his. Then I had the stores save theirs for me. You should have seen all the cigar boxes I had. They were piled up in the closet and under my bed and stacked in the corners. You wouldn't believe how many I had."

"Oh, yes I would, Steve," she replied solemnly. "When did you give up the collection—just before you moved here?"

"That's right," he replied good-naturedly. "How did you guess?"

"Knowing you, it was pretty easy."

"Seriously, Janet . . ."

"When have we ever been serious?"

"Not too often, I guess. Now, what *are* you going to do with the boxes?"

Janet looked down at the round wooden lid, then touched the tip of the tiny brush to a vine. Actually, until Steve had pressed the matter, she hadn't thought about it. She had fallen into the habit of making the boxes when she had nothing else to do. "Maybe I'll start selling them," she announced. "If I keep it up, I should have lots by next Christmas. I'll advertise in the local newspaper: 'The perfect Christmas gift—enameled boxes—Janet Lindquist Originals.' How much you think I should ask for them?"

She held out the lid for Steve's inspection. He glared at it, and at her. Instead of answering her, he paced across the room again.

"What's the matter with you?" she wanted to know. "You're pacing around like a caged tiger."

"That's only because I feel like one."

"What's the matter?"

He glared again, then turned his scowl toward the front window. The drapes were open to reveal the blanket of snow across the lawn. It had been beautiful when it had first fallen a week or so ago. Now it was gray and grimy-looking, well tracked and worn from all the snowball fights and snowman making. The snowplows had been down the street and piled the snow up along the sides. It made it better for traffic, of course, but it didn't improve the scenery to have banks of dirty, hard snow. Ever since it had fallen, the temperature had remained too cold for the snow and ice to melt. It became uglier every day.

"I never thought," Steve grumbled, "that I would wish that Christmas vacation was over and that school would start, but I am so sick of this weather and being stuck inside. I don't see how you can stand to sit there and play with those boring boxes. It drives me crazy just to watch you."

Janet stared up at him in mild surprise. It was on the tip of her tongue to tell him he didn't have to watch, he could go home. However, she had been so relieved when he had shown up after the Christmas-night party at his house and acted like her pal again that she didn't want to make him mad. If she annoyed him, he just might tease her about the kisses under the mistletoe and that was an episode she was trying hard to forget.

"Well, Stephen, if you want me to do something else, just say so. You don't have to make mean remarks about my hobby. But what are we going to do? We've worn most of the snow off the good sledding hills. Besides, I'm sick of playing in the snow. Even if I weren't, it's too frozen and dirty to do much with. My parents won't let me drive at all. *Yours* won't let you drive anything but the Scout and your dad took it to work."

He shrugged his broad shoulders and looked downcast. "There has to be *something*. Maybe we could walk to town?" he suggested hopefully.

"It's two degrees below zero out there," she said. "And it's a *long* way to town. Would you settle for some hot chocolate and a game of Scrabble?"

"I hate Scrabble," he said flatly.

"But *I* like it. Why do we always have to play the games *you* pick?"

He narrowed his eyes speculatively and Janet tried not to think about how cute he looked. "Okay, Lindquist, I'll make a deal with you. Walk to town and back with me. Afterwards, I'll play Scrabble until *you're* ready to call it quits. How's that?"

"We'll freeze," she protested, glancing out at the gloomy sky and gray-white mounds of snow. Maybe what she was doing wasn't exactly exciting but it *was* cozy. A fire was roaring in the fireplace and she was dressed warmly in a sweat shirt, corduroy pants, and her fuzzy blue slippers.

"Sissy," he accused. "Where's your pioneer spirit?"

"If I ever had any, it got up and left," she replied. "Steve, you can't be serious. I keep telling you . . . it's *cold* out there."

"If we bundle up like Eskimos, we won't even feel it. Really, Janet, you're beginning to act more like your sister and her friends. Suggest walking or something a little different to that bunch and they freak out."

That did it. If there was anything Janet couldn't stand, it was to be told she was acting like Michelle. Steve probably knew that, which was why he'd said it. However, it worked and she rose to the bait.

"Okay, Steve. You win. You go round up your Eskimo suit and I'll see what I can find to put on. This is probably going to turn out to be the dumbest thing I've ever done in my entire life. I mean, they'll probably find our frozen bodies in the spring. There are drifts out there so deep that if we were accidentally buried, not even the Saint Bernards could find us."

He raised his eyebrows comically. "Between here and Main Street? Not likely we'll get lost. And if we do, we shouldn't be stuck for more than a month or two."

"That's a comforting thought," she said with a grin. "Well, beat it, buddy. Let's get this show on the road. If I don't do it now, I'll change my mind. That roaring fire feels awfully good."

"Then think how much better it will feel after you've walked to town and back."

"I'd rather not think about it," she grumbled.

After Steve had gone, she went to her room. Starting with insulated underwear, she put on nearly every warm garment she owned. She was so bundled up that her legs and arms almost couldn't bend.

"Goodness," Nancy said when she saw Janet walking

down the hall. "You look as if you've gained thirty pounds."

"Don't worry, Mom. I've been hitting the fudge, but not that heavily. Most of this will come off when I undress. Steve and I are walking to town."

"You'll freeze."

"That's what I told him."

"And you're going anyway? Must be true love."

"Mom," she replied impatiently, "I wish you'd quit saying stuff like that. I think I've told this family at least a million times that Steve Wayman and I—"

"I was only kidding," Nancy interrupted gently. "I know you're just good friends and I think that's fine. Have a good time, keep your mittens on, and wear a muffler so you can put it across your face when you're against the wind. I don't want to have to be driving through this to find a doctor to treat frostbite."

"Your concern is touching," Janet joked, then waddled away when the doorbell rang.

Steve laughed out loud at her bundled appearance and awkward movements. "You walk like a penguin," he told her.

"You think you look better?" she asked, her eyes moving down the thick, insulated coverall and stocking cap.

"Who's worried about looks? Ready, partner?"

"Ready," she said with a sigh, shivering with dread when he threw open the door and nudged her out into the subzero weather that was edged in dampness.

As Steve had told her, it wasn't really *that* bad. With as many layers of clothing as they wore, it would take the cold a long, long time to chill them thoroughly. They moved as quickly as possible but movements were impeded by the combination of ice, drifts, heavy boots, and too much clothing. Steve's long legs carried him over and through places that were difficult for Janet to overcome. Time after time she fell into the drifts. Sometimes she struggled up by herself. Sometimes Steve pulled her up.

"You know, Lindquist," he said when he assisted her out of still another drift, "we'll accomplish this expedition a lot faster if you'd manage to stay on your feet."

"I know," she said with a giggle. "You know something, Steve, it's so hard for me to move my legs with all this nonsense on that I'm beginning to *feel* like a penguin. Waddle, waddle, waddle. That's all I can do."

"Then I'll waddle with you," he said cheerfully.

They were along Elm Street. Cars and trucks passed occasionally, but Janet and Steve were too busy trying to stand up to pay much attention to the traffic. Steve took the lead, walking with a silly waddling gait that made him look exactly like a huge penguin. Giggling helplessly, Janet followed him.

"I don't look that silly," she called ahead to him.

"Wanna bet?" he called back over his shoulder. All that showed were his wide grin and very red cheeks.

He continued his waddle and Janet did her best to be a better penguin than he was. When he reached back and took her hand, she didn't protest. The sidewalk was icy and treacherous. Side by side instead of single file, they continued their penguin imitations down Elm Street. Janet looked out at the street. A familiar-looking red four-wheel-drive truck was coming toward them.

"Don't look now," she muttered, "but here come Jordan and Michelle. The Preppy Pair."

"Who cares? I bet we're having more fun than they are."

Janet looked up at the truck and waved merrily. Michelle waved back, but Janet didn't miss seeing that her sister rolled her eyes upward in exasperation. Michelle was wearing her new blush and lipstick that complemented the puffy lilac coat she had gotten for Christmas. Jordan looked very mature and sophisticated in his Fair Isle sweater. Undoubtedly Michelle found it a bit embarrassing for her college boyfriend to know she had a sister who did penguin imitations right out in public.

"We're almost there," Steve said, squeezing her hand. She could feel the pressure of the squeeze through the padding provided by his gloves and hers. "We'll stop in at Casey's and I'll buy you some hot chocolate or coffee."

"That's big of you."

"I try to be generous to the little people in life."

She kicked at his leg and missed. She was so bundled up that she couldn't do anything right. Not only did she miss his leg, but she slipped and would have fallen into another drift if he hadn't caught her by the wrists and pulled her up. When she was more or less solidly on her feet, he let go of her. She was surprised at how suddenly lonely she was. He was still right there, of course, but she missed the comfort of his hand over hers.

"Listen, twerp, try that again and I'll back out on the hot drink."

"So?" she said. "I imagine Michelle and Jordan were headed home. I'll just call from Casey's and have Jordan come get me in his big red truck. Then you'll have to walk home alone."

He dropped down on his knees in the snow and peered up at her in mock alarm. "Oh, please, no. Don't make me find my way home alone. Together we might have a chance. Alone . . . well, as you said, there would be nothing left but a skeleton by the time the Saint Bernards found me."

"Okay. I'm a sympathetic person. Throw in a cheeseburger and I'll stick with you."

"A cheeseburger?" he asked with great indignation. "Gold digger."

"All of this fresh air and exercise has given me an appetite. If you don't have enough money, I brought a little. It's here somewhere."

Her feet began to slip again as she hunted about for the right pocket.

"That's all right," Steve said quickly, laughing at her. "Hunting out your money could be hazardous to both of us.

Look, here we are already. I can see Casey's in the next block. See it?"

Janet put her mittened hand to her forehead and pretended to peer out across a blizzard-stricken horizon. "By George, Wayman, I think we've found civilization. Think the natives will speak English?"

"We can only try. If not, we'll use sign language."

She tugged at his coverall sleeve. "Hey, quick, tell me what the sign is for cheeseburger."

"Food, food, food. That's all you ever think about."

"That isn't true. Sometimes I think about sleep."

"And little wooden boxes."

Giggling and stumbling, they made their way into the little restaurant and sat down in a booth. It was too much trouble to take off much, but they did remove their caps and mittens. After their order had been taken, an argument began over who had the reddest nose. When the waitress returned with the huge burgers and steaming cups of hot chocolate, Steve asked her, "Would you mind doing us a favor?"

" 'Course not," replied the gum-chewing waitress.

"We're having this really serious discussion," he continued, "and we need an impartial party for some objective input."

The girl's eyes narrowed with suspicion and she shifted from one foot to the other. She had obviously been expecting to be asked to bring another bottle of catsup or some similar duty. "Look . . ." she began.

Steve held up a hand and gave her his totally beguiling grin. The waitress halted her protest and waited for him to finish. Janet took careful note of the incident. Apparently she wasn't the only female who found Steve Wayman's charm irresistible.

"All we need for you to do is say which one of us has the reddest nose. That's all. No pressure. No feedback. Just state your honest opinion, then I won't keep you from your duties. Please believe that I truly want you to be impartial in your decision. Don't let the fact that *I'm* paying the check and will be leaving the tip—if there is one—sway you at all."

The waitress adjusted the ties on her apron, then giggled like the teenager she had been only a few short years ago. "Well, in that case, I'll try hard to be fair and impartial. *Your* nose is definitely redder than hers. Most definitely."

"That's what I thought," he said with a quick, happy laugh. "Thanks for your time and patience. It will be well rewarded." To add to the foolishness, he waved a nickel in front of her.

Before she walked off, she shook her head and said, "The last of the big spenders. You know, on second thought, your girl's nose is redder. This fluorescent lighting had me fooled for a moment."

Janet looked over at Steve. She was laughing so hard that she couldn't speak for a moment. When she did recover, she said, "Does that mean I get the nickel? After all, she certainly didn't seem to appreciate it."

He shoved the nickel firmly back down in his pocket. "No way. I'm beginning to think the female sex is completely money-hungry and without any sense of appreciation for the small things in life."

"Such as your small tips. And your even smaller jokes," Janet quipped.

Steve bit into his burger and pretended to ignore her. In fact, he was acting very sophisticated until a piece of onion dropped onto his chin and stuck there. When Janet laughed at him and reached across the table to remove the onion with a napkin, he gave up the charade and joined her in laughter.

"You know something, Wayman," she said between bites, "you've definitely been around me too much. You're even taking up my bad habits."

"Such as?" he asked with an air of innocence.

"Ah, come on. When you first moved to Barkley and were dating Michelle, would you honestly have stopped a waitress and asked her to be a judge in a red nose contest?"

He gave the question careful consideration. "Well, frankly, my dear, no. You've taught me a lot about loosening up and having fun and not caring so much what other people think. You're pretty special, Janet."

"And that's the truth?"

"It sure is," he stated, giving her a look that was a bit too serious and sentimental.

Janet ducked her head, acted as if she hadn't seen the look, and, very quickly, said, "You've even been seen in the main part of town doing a penguin imitation. Think of the shame."

"I never thought about it, but you're right. I guess I'll just have to leave town and never show my face again," Steve said, wiping away an imaginary tear.

Giggling slightly, Janet drained the last bit of warm chocolate from the heavy mug. Their food was nearly gone. Between it and the laughter, she felt snugly warm and serene. She wished moments like these could go on forever, that life itself could be composed of such moments . . . one after the other, all connected in a bright patchwork design. Steve was such a marvelous guy. She had never known anyone who was as much fun to be with. Taking a quick glance at his handsome features and shining hair and eyes, she found herself wishing he were just a little bit homely. But he wasn't. He was completely gorgeous. And that was the trouble. He was such a hunk that it was only a matter of time before some cute girl grabbed him up and he'd be back playing the dating game again, too busy to indulge in adolescent nonsense with his next-door neighbor.

"Hey, you're quiet all of a sudden. What are you thinking about?"

Janet hoped she was still red enough from the cold that he couldn't see the slight blush she felt steal over her face. Since he so obviously regarded her as a good friend, there was no way she could tell him what she had been thinking. He might realize she cared about him.

"Just about life," she answered carefully.

"Hmmm. That is a *big* subject."

"Ain't it, though? I think you'd better put your nickel back on the table so we can bundle up again and start the weary trek homeward. After all, the Scrabble board awaits you."

Steve curled his upper lip comically. "Scrabble? You must be out of your mind. I don't play Scrabble."

"You promised."

"Did you get it in writing?"

"No, but I did get it on the tape recorder."

"I never suspected your place was bugged," Steve said, pretending to be shocked.

"Most people don't. Not even my dad. And don't tell him. He'll have the exterminator in right away."

"Smart man. Most *normal* people don't like living with bugs."

"But then I've been told I'm not terribly normal," she said cheerfully, standing up to give the muffler one last wrap around her neck.

"You've been told right, Janet."

She smiled sweetly as they walked out into the cold air once more. "Insult me if you want, Steve, but you'll eat your words once I've beaten you in Scrabble."

Steve just laughed. His laughter seemed to reach out and touch the cold air, to put a ray of sunshine into the otherwise bleak sky, and to create a glow within Janet that made her uncomfortable.

She kept telling herself that she regarded him only as a friend. Now, however, she was beginning to wonder if she would ever manage to convince herself.

It wasn't going to be easy.

Chapter Six

"Really, Janet, you must have cast a spell over Steve," said Michelle.

It was very near bedtime and the four Lindquists sat lazily before the fire, which was slowly dying. As the flames became smaller and less ferocious, the members of the family began to yawn. One yawn led to another, spreading contagiously.

Janet wiggled her toes inside her fuzzy slippers and didn't respond to Michelle's comment. She had had her fill of trying to explain her relationship with Steve to her family. She wasn't trying anymore.

Michelle, however, wasn't easily discouraged. "I never thought I'd see the day Steve Wayman would waddle like an idiot down one of the main streets in town, then spend the rest of the evening playing Scrabble like a good little boy. It doesn't fit his image."

Janet shrugged. "You sure of that, Michelle? Maybe you just look at the outsides of people and decide what their 'images' should be when what they are inside isn't like that 'image' at all."

Roger's sleepy eyes flew open and he looked at Janet in surprise. "That's a very astute comment, Janet. You're a good judge of human nature."

"Could be," she agreed cheerfully. "Everyone keeps telling me we all have talents. Maybe that's mine. With a little work maybe I could make a fortune as a personnel director for some big company."

"Before the plans get too big," Nancy said with a yawn, "I think this bunch better go to bed."

"By the way, Michelle," Janet said as she piled the pillows back onto the sofa, "we weren't waddling like idiots. That wouldn't be dignified. We were merely doing penguin imitations."

Michelle shook her head and looked at Janet in grudging admiration. "Then you've cast an even bigger spell than I thought. You've definitely got a catch there."

Janet glared at her sister but didn't bother to reply.

"I know, I know," Michelle said with a sleepy little laugh, "and maybe that's what you really think: just friends. But I've got some advice for you, baby sister. If you like Steve, wake up and see things the way they are. That guy could date any girl in town. He hangs around with you because he *wants* to. Press the good buddy bit too far and too long and he'll give up."

Anger flared up in Janet. If her parents hadn't been there, she would have told her sister a few things. However, not wanting to cause a family war right at bedtime on a cold, wintry night, she settled for giving Michelle a long, cool stare, then said, "If you persist in misunderstanding the situation, there's nothing I can do. But I will tell you that you're wrong about one thing. You say Steve can date any girl in town. He can't. *I* wouldn't date him. Be his friend, yes. But date him, no. And quite obviously, he can't date you, either. Or have you changed your mind, Michelle?"

Without waiting for a reply, Janet turned and went off to her room.

As she lay in bed, it occurred to her that Michelle *did* seem overly interested in Steve's relationship with her. Maybe Michelle was beginning to regret what she had thrown away. Jordan had already gone back to college. Besides, all he had going for him was his age. *Anyone* could tell that Steve was better-looking. He was also nicer, funnier, smarter, and a better athlete. By himself Jordan was all right. Next to Steve he suddenly looked like a stick figure.

The thought that Michelle might want Steve back wasn't an appealing one. In fact, it made her stomach churn. All along she had *known* that Steve liked Michelle better than he liked her. Or, anyway, in a different way. He liked Janet in a friend-to-friend way, but he liked Michelle in a boy-to-girl way that was completely separate. He had been hanging around the house an awful lot lately. Well, maybe it was beginning to pay off. Michelle sure was noticing him. Hardly a day went by that she didn't mention him in some way.

Janet's thoughts weren't happy ones. The contented feeling she'd had all day had vanished and she felt lonely and cold in the dark room. She remembered the cold nights when, as very little children, she and Michelle would take turns sleeping in each other's rooms. That time seemed very far away. Janet tried to imagine going into Michelle's room and saying, "I'm cold. Move over. Let's take turns saying what we'd do if we had a million dollars. You go first. We'll quit when we get sleepy."

Her heart felt like a lump of lead. Another lump formed in her throat. She was close to crying and she didn't even know *why*. It was dumb, so very dumb.

Life had been so much simpler when she and Michelle were little. That had been before boys, bras, dances, dates, makeup, and beauty contests. They had had arguments then, too, of course, but they had been brief and easily settled. Janet could remember her mother putting an arm around each angry girl and hugging them, then proceeding to straighten out the terrible problem of whom the blue-sequined Barbie-doll gown really belonged to. Back then, Janet had felt good when Mom had said, "Red hair, black hair, blond hair. It doesn't make any difference. Just keep it clean and shiny and neat and be proud of what you are. It would be a boring world if we were all alike. I love you each the way you are."

Those words had comforted Janet when she was seven years old. The memory of them wasn't much comfort now. Sure, *Mom* loved them both the way they were and her love *was* important. But the trouble with mothers is that they always love their kids the way they are even if they're cross-eyed and have warts. But boys like Steve Wayman weren't too keen on crossed eyes and warts. Or even on red hair and freckles. They liked tall, willowy creatures with smooth, shining hair. Girls like Michelle Lindquist.

Janet stretched her legs and yawned. Boys. They weren't worth the trouble they caused. Not even Steve Wayman. If he was just being her friend because he hoped to get close to Michelle again, she might as well find it out. Tomorrow she was going to find a way to tell Steve she thought Michelle was interested in him again. His reaction to that bit of news ought to be amusing. Or maybe *amusing* wasn't the right word. She didn't need a crystal ball to tell her she wouldn't be amused if Steve leaped at the chance to date her sister again.

Finally, in spite of her unhappiness, Janet grew drowsy, and soon her worries were temporarily soothed away by a deep, peaceful sleep.

Bright and early the next morning, long before she was ready to wake up, Janet's mother nudged her gently on the shoulder and told her she had a telephone call. Janet glanced at the clock and wondered who got up this early when there was no school. Wrapping her robe around her, she stumbled to the telephone. If it was Steve Wayman, she was going to kill him for waking her up. The flash of disappointment she felt when she heard Kay's voice in response to her own

"Hello" was troubling. She hid that feeling, more for her own benefit than for Kay's, by saying cheerily, "Hey, it's great to hear from you. I thought maybe you had become permanently snowbound."

"And you were so worried you hadn't even called to check," Kay replied. She didn't sound bitter. She was just stating a fact. However, the truth of that fact hit home. Janet *had* been neglecting her friends.

"I meant to call," she said lamely. "I really did, but time has just gotten away from me. I can't believe we go back to school Monday. Seems like we just got out."

"Don't worry about it," Kay told her. "If I had someone as cute as Steve Wayman hanging around all the time, I don't suppose I'd think much about calling *girls* either."

"Don't tell me I'm going to have to explain all this to you again, too," Janet said, giving a laugh that didn't quite ring true. "You know how it is with Steve and me."

"I know," her friend replied in a way that let Janet think she just might know more than Janet wanted her to.

"Anyway, Kay, what's up?"

"Not a lot. Just a case of cabin fever, I guess. The county didn't get around to clearing off our road until late yesterday. Dad feels sorry for me, I think, because I haven't been able to get out at all since the snow, so he said I could drive our four-wheeler into town today. I didn't even ask. I just wondered if you'd want to do something. If you didn't have other plans, that is."

Janet thought for a moment, her still sleepy mind trying to reach back to yesterday to remember if Steve had mentioned doing anything. Suddenly she was wide-awake and angry with herself. Steve, Steve, Steve. He was becoming an obsession with her. It had to end. There was no way she was going to plan all her activities around what Steve said or didn't say.

"Of course I don't have other plans. What time can you be over?"

The girls talked for a few minutes while they made their plans. Janet then decided she had time to go back to bed for a while. She slipped under the covers and alternated between sleeping and reading until it was time to get up. While she was in the kitchen eating a sandwich, Steve burst in the back door. He knocked, of course, but then came on in without waiting for a response.

"Want something to eat?" she asked without looking up.

"What are you having?"

She glanced down at the thick sandwich and tried to recall its ingredients. "Spam, bologna, tomato, dill pickle, two kinds of cheese, peanut butter, and a sliced-up boiled egg."

"Uh, no thanks. It sounds lethal."

"And filled with calories," Nancy put in sternly from where she was unloading the dishwasher.

Janet shook her head. She told Steve, "Mom never gives up on her attempts to reform me. She keeps wanting me to be a slender model instead of my chubby self."

Nancy looked at her in surprise. "Why, I've never said you were chubby, dear."

"Then why all the talk about calories all the time?"

"Because you're just right and I want you to stay that way. 'Just right' has a way of turning into 'chubby' if you aren't on guard. Believe me, I know," she said as she made a face and patted her own hips. "But right now, you have a very nice figure. Doesn't she, Steve?"

He looked embarrassed as he slid into the chair across from Janet. "She looks okay to me," he mumbled, "but what do I know about girls? Peanut butter with Spam and pickles? I can't believe . . ."

Janet calmly lifted up the layers of bread to reveal the contents of the sandwich to Steve. He shuddered at the sight.

"Have a banana or an apple instead," she said, sliding a bowl of fruit across the table.

He took an apple and bit into the bright-red skin. "Ready for another walk today?" he asked.

"Where did you have in mind this time, Admiral Byrd?" she asked wryly.

"Thought we might go a few miles due west. I heard of a penguin colony up that way that needs investigating."

"Sorry, but you'll have to go it alone. Kay's coming in and I'm going to spend some time goofing around with her."

Steve actually looked disappointed. Janet fought down the urge to ask him to join them. Kay might not like the idea. Besides, she felt she needed a little time away from Steve to sort out some weird ideas she had been having. Who knows? She might even get up enough courage to tell Kay her problem. Some good old-fashioned girl talk couldn't hurt at this point.

"Oh, well," he said at last. "I guess I'll hunt up Chuck or Tim or some of the guys. Go to the arcade and see what's cooking. Maybe I'll give you a call tonight if we both get in before too late."

Janet's answering nod was noncommittal.

He got up and walked over to the door. For a few moments, he just stood there looking back at her. Aware of his contemplation of her, Janet looked down at her navy sweater and brushed away some crumbs.

"Is something wrong, Steve?" she asked.

"That's just what I was wondering. You seem in a funny mood."

"Me?" she inquired, lifting her eyebrows and wiggling them at him in her best Groucho Marx imitation. "Never."

"I hope not," he said with a laugh. "See you later."

"If you're lucky, that is."

He glared at her through the pane of glass in the kitchen door as he closed it behind him. With the frosty pane between them, Janet wiggled her eyebrows again and watched his answering smile. He laughed again. She couldn't hear the sound of that laughter but she knew it was there. No matter how old she got or how far away she moved, she would never forget the sound of Steve's laughter.

She was glad when Kay finally arrived and they were able to escape her mother's worried dos and don'ts about driving around on the icy streets.

"I'll go real slow, Mrs. Lindquist," Kay assured.

Once out on the treacherous streets in the Bronco, Janet quickly became convinced that slow was the only way to go. She was glad that Kay showed no signs of wanting to get adventurous.

"It isn't that I've gotten so cautious and wise," explained Kay with a sigh. "It's just that I know if I end up in a mess, I'll never get this chance again."

"I hate to tell you this, friend, but thinking like that *is* cautious and wise. But I'm not knocking it. Why spoil a good thing?"

They talked, giggled, and exchanged gossip. When they were tired of driving up and down the icy streets, they went to a fast-food restaurant to get something to eat.

"You see much of Ronnie these days?" Janet asked, nibbling at a French fry.

"Now and then. Not as much as I did there for a while," Kay confided, "but that's really okay. I mean, Ronnie's a nice guy and all, but I'm beginning to think it would be nice to date other fellows. It's kind of dumb to get serious, don't you think?"

Janet thought about it. She had known both Ronnie and Kay all of her life. It was rather hard to imagine them being serious about each other. Instead of saying that, however, she said, "Yeah, I guess it would be. Plenty of fish in the sea and all those other platitudes. Playing the field. Fish playing the field. Doesn't make sense, does it?"

"That's all right," Kay replied with a laugh. "You don't make any more sense when you talk than you ever did."

"And heaven forbid that I should ever begin making sense," Janet avowed.

"Amen. But then, you don't make sense in other ways. You advise to play the field, then *you* stay in the same corner all the time."

"Meaning what?" Janet asked, eyes narrowed with suspicion.

"Steve. What else?"

Janet gave a sigh. She looked over her friend's round, merry face carefully and made her decision: she would confide in Kay. If she didn't talk to *someone* about this, she would go crazy.

"Okay, Kay, you seem determined to talk about this. Prepared to give me a little advice?"

"I don't know. Are you prepared to take any?" her friend challenged.

"That depends on if I like it or not."

Kay shrugged. "I guess we're all that way. Is this like third grade and I have to make a blood oath not to tell another single living soul?"

Janet nodded. "I'd also prefer it if you wouldn't tell a single dead soul, either. Okay?"

"Sounds like a safe-enough promise."

"Not only do you keep insisting that Steve and I are an 'item,' so does my whole family. We never really 'date,' Kay. We really don't. Am I *that* obvious? I mean, can everyone *tell* how I feel about him?"

Kay nodded sympathetically. "To me, it shows. But then, I've known you forever. I saw the look on your face when you had it bad for our eighth-grade science teacher."

"And I look that way *now?*"

"More or less. Only it's more more than less."

"I don't think he likes me that way, Kay. To him I'm not a girl, just a good buddy. That's why I don't want it to be so obvious that I love him."

"You have to take a chance on things sometimes," Kay said slowly. "I mean, if you do love him, you ought to let him know. You can't be sure he doesn't feel the same way you do. Personally, I don't think he'd spend as much time with you as he does if he didn't like you a lot and think you're special."

"But he never says . . . I mean, he never really *asks* for a date like most boys would. He just shows up and . . ."

"Maybe you don't give him a chance," Kay said gently. "Remember when Jim was trying to ask you to that dance and you kept making jokes and all that until he lost his courage and gave up? I think you're doing the same thing with Steve."

"It's possible," Janet admitted, "but . . ."

"But *what?*"

Then Janet blurted out the long, troubled story of how she couldn't rid herself of the feeling that Steve was just using her so that he would be there handy when Michelle decided to give him another chance. "And I think she's beginning to want him back," she finished breathlessly.

Kay gave her a long, careful look and shook her head. "How could you love a guy if you thought he was the kind to 'use' you that way?"

"That's how it gets all mixed up. He's *not* that type. He's a really nice guy and I think he does like me, but I want him to more than like me and he can't help it if he's all hung up on Michelle."

"Then tell him you think she likes him again and see what he does."

Janet swallowed hard. "I thought about that. I'm not sure I'm ready to take that chance."

"And so we're back to 'chances.' You gotta take chances, Janet. I never dated a boy until Ronnie asked me out. He didn't date much before me, either. Only now I'm beginning to not like the being-attached-to-just-one feeling. If I tell him that—and I'm going to—then I'm taking a chance on no dates at all. But the thing is, Ronnie and I can't just stay stuck to each other because we're both afraid no one else will ever want us. We're too young for that. Besides, at any age, that would be dumb. Just both being rejects isn't having a lot in common."

"You're not a reject," Janet protested.

"I think I know that now, but you get my drift? You won't

date *any* boy in town because you think they all like Michelle better."

"Well, they all do," she said stubbornly.

"You can't know that. Sure, she's pretty and popular and real outgoing and you're sort of hard to get to know, but you're lots of fun when you do open up. But that's the thing: you have to open up. I know it's not the same with you and me as it is with you and Steve. Yet, in a way, it is. I know you're my friend. I have no doubts about that, so I feel okay about calling you and coming by your house and talking to you about things that bother me, but if you kept a curtain up all the time, I couldn't do that."

Kay's confusing explanation almost made Janet's head hurt. Kay, however, had no mercy.

"So that's how it has to be with a guy. With Steve, of course, in your case. If he knows you like him in a special way, then he might start acting more like a regular date than a buddy, but you won't know if you don't—"

"Take a chance," Janet said, finishing the sentence for her. "But if I let him know I care for him, then it might scare him off. I'd rather have his friendship than not see him at all."

"Are you sure about that?" Kay asked shrewdly. "Seems to me you've gotten to the point where you're as miserable as you are happy. Having it out in the open might be a relief."

Janet was still wary. "But I don't want to lose . . ." she began, then hesitated.

Kay shrugged and sipped her soda. "Life's a game," she said philosophically, "and there's no way to get out of playing it. Except by dying and who's in any hurry for that? And you know how games are . . . you lose a few. On the other hand, you win a few."

"That's deep, friend," Janet said with a laugh. "Real deep."

"I know. I'm becoming a very profound thinker. Gonna do it?"

"I'm going to think about it," Janet hedged.

"Deeply?"

"And profoundly," she promised.

Kay replied, "I guess I'll settle for that, then."

They didn't return to the subject the rest of the day, but Janet's mind didn't leave it. The thoughts were there and overrode everything else in her mind.

Chapter Seven

"Janet. Yoo-hoo! Are you in there, Janet?"

From where she sat cross-legged on the floor, Janet blinked, then glared at Steve. They sat on the Lindquist carpet, the battered Scrabble board between them, and were in the last stages of the game when they each had only a few remaining tiles. It was Janet's turn. She was supposed to be concentrating on how to get rid of the *Z* she possessed. Instead, she was concentrating on the talk she and Kay had had the day before.

"Quit waving your arms around in front of me, Stephen," she said irritably. "I'm trying to think."

"*Think?* You looked more like you had gone into a trance. If your eyes hadn't been open, I would have sworn you were asleep. Just as blank as blank can be. No thought processes at all."

"Shows how much you know about anything," she replied with a sniff. "The sleeping mind isn't a blank. The subconscious mind is always at work."

His gray-blue eyes held a twinkle as he grinned at her

across the tile-filled game board. "There are exceptions to all rules, Lindquist. And I think *your* mind is the exception. If anything could be a total blank, it could."

Instead of making some clever reply, she looked at him more closely. He had such fantastic eyes, sort of a smoky color, set off by thick, dark lashes.

"Janet," he said softly, breaking into her thoughts. "You've gone away on me again. I said I'd play Scrabble until you were ready to beg for mercy. Looks now as if the game is boring *you*. And just when I was getting addicted to it."

"Who says I'm bored?" Janet asked indignantly. "Watch this."

A quick glance across the board located a place she had managed to miss. Where a *D* ended one word and an *E* began another, there were two vacant spaces. With a triumphant flourish, she moved an *O* and her hateful *Z* into place.

"I don't believe it. I just don't believe it. I would have sworn your mind was a million miles off and you go and take the place I had picked for my turn."

"Just play. I think it's your turn now."

A million miles off? she thought. Not exactly. More like a few inches.

When the game was finally ended, however, Janet did admit she had had her fill of Scrabble. Steve eagerly took the game and returned it to the hall closet. He placed it on the highest shelf on the very top of a tall stack of other games.

"Hey, I can't reach it there. What did you put it way up there for?"

"Out of sight, out of mind. If it's up where you can't see it or reach it, then maybe I won't get roped into playing for a while."

She stretched out on the carpet, wiggling her toes inside the fuzzy slippers. She was wearing baggy maroon sweat pants that Nancy had accidentally sprinkled a little liquid bleach on. "They look like they have leprosy," Janet had exclaimed in delight and, to her mother's dismay, had continued to wear them on every possible occasion. With the sweat pants, she wore a faded flannel shirt of her father's; its tapered tails flopped about her hips. If she was serious about changing her relationship with Steve, she mused, then perhaps she really should dress better. Her mind rejected that thought immediately. She didn't want things to change *that* much. All she wanted was for them to stay just like they were—only better. Not even for Steve could she dress in lace and ruffles. Besides, he'd probably laugh his head off if she tried.

Returning to the subject at hand, she said, "It isn't fair, you know, to take advantage of your height. Tall people are so boring. Always lording it over the average citizen as if height in itself gives some special license."

He stretched out on the floor beside her, his frame taking up nearly a foot more than hers did.

"Far be it from me to lord it over anyone for any reason. See, I'm even stooping to your level. Don't be so defensive because you're a Munchkin. It isn't something you had a choice about, I suppose."

Glaring at him, Janet rolled over and began to pound him lightly on the chest. Laughing, he took both of her hands in his and pushed her back until she was again lying on the floor and he was hovering inches away from her face.

"Munchkins are noted for their bravery," he said, still holding her in place though she struggled, "if not for their intelligence. In moments of great anger, plucky little Munchkins have been known to attack beings twice their size. Alas, they have frequently had cause to regret this."

"I'm not a Munchkin. And you're not twice my size," she protested. While she spoke, she tried to free her hands from his grasp but he kept them tightly imprisoned. "Let me go, Stephen Wayman!"

"Beg me," he taunted. His eyes twinkled down at her, their corners all crinkly with laughter and she couldn't really get angry. He was teasing her with open affection, not with hatefulness.

"Never in a hundred million years," she vowed.

"Then only one thing else can save you," he warned.

"What's that?"

His expression underwent a subtle change and Janet wasn't sure she wanted an answer to her question. He bent his head closer toward hers. He's going to kiss me, she realized. Immediately she was seized with panic and indecision. Should she let him? Should she fight him? If she let him, how should she act? Should she kiss him back or just remain passive and act like it didn't affect her at all? Should she make some wisecrack afterwards? She couldn't afford to let this situation get too serious.

Steve's head moved again. There was a funny expression in his eyes and his lips were slightly parted. He's going to kiss me all right, she thought. His face was a disturbingly short distance away from hers.

"You two at it again? This time it's a wrestling match, no less. With you two around, the house is like a perpetual kindergarten," said Michelle in a superior-sounding voice.

Steve instantly released Janet's hands and fell back on the floor. Janet rolled over on her stomach, propped her elbows on the floor to make a resting place for her chin, and regarded her older sister carefully.

"In my opinion, dear sister, a perpetual kindergarten beats the heck out of a perpetual Miss America pageant."

Her tone wasn't exactly friendly. Michelle, who had been joking, looked at Janet with widened eyes. "What's that supposed to mean?"

"Only that you don't seem real. Not you or anything you do. You and your boyfriends—and precious Jordan is the worst—are like . . . well, like Barbie and Ken. Dressing up and acting cool and being afraid to relax and act like real people because of 'what people might think.' It makes me sick. It really does."

Michelle's eyes continued to widen under Janet's spontaneous attack.

"Watch it, Michelle," Janet couldn't refrain from saying. "Your eyelashes are going to go all the way up and get stuck against your eyebrows. With all that goop on, you may never get them unstuck again. Think of trying to sleep with your eyes glued wide open. Couldn't be too comfortable."

"Listen, Janet, knock it off," Michelle said. "I didn't mean anything by what I said. There's no reason to get so nasty."

Janet looked up at her sister. Maybe there *wasn't* any reason to get so nasty. Somehow Michelle always brought out the worst in her. The way her sister looked standing there in her designer jeans and pastel sweater didn't help the situation. After all, Steve was looking at Michelle, too. He had been nearly ready to kiss *her* until they had been interrupted and now his eyes were focused on Michelle, with her long, shining hair caught back in a clasp at the nape of her neck and with just enough makeup to highlight her pretty features.

Janet reflected on her recent conversation with Kay. Telling Steve that she thought Michelle was interested in him again to get his reaction wouldn't be necessary. She was witnessing his reaction to Michelle. All her sister had to do was smile and crook her little finger and she would be back riding around with Steve in his Camaro again while Janet went back to painting whimsical unicorns and daydreaming about what it would be like to get away from Barkley.

"Michelle's right," Steve said gently, tearing his gaze away from Michelle's face long enough to look down at Janet and place a hand on her shoulder. She felt her shoulder stiffen involuntarily in reaction to his touch. She didn't want him touching her at all. Not if he was still mooning over Michelle . . . and it was pretty obvious that he was. "I think she just meant to kid us but the steam started coming out of your ears right away."

"Of course Michelle is right," Janet said stonily. "Michelle is always right. You have my apologies, dear sister, if I've offended you in any way. Now, if you'll excuse me, I'm going to my room. I need to see if I can find some corks for my ears to keep the steam from escaping. Perhaps I can channel the steam inside and use it as a source of energy for my brain. It needs all the assistance it can get."

With those words, she got up and strode across the room with all the dignity her homely outfit and ridiculous speech would allow.

"Hey, Janet," Steve called to her back. He sounded surprised. "Come on back here. Let's talk about this."

"Talk?" She turned slightly and gave him the most withering glance she had at her command. "There's nothing to talk about. For a while, I thought you were different, but you're not. I mean, you may be different but you don't really want to be. You just want to be another Ken. Just waiting for the chance. Outside you may look cool, Steve Wayman, but inside you're pure polyester."

"That's a rotten thing to say," he said, jumping to his feet and glaring at her.

She shrugged diffidently, gave him one last look, and said, "The truth's the truth." With those words, she retreated to her room.

Before she got completely away, however, she heard Michelle say in a bewildered voice, "Pure polyester inside? What on earth does she mean by that, Steve?"

"You have to know how Janet's mind works to understand," he began.

She kept on going. If they were going to discuss her, she didn't want to hear it. If Michelle was going to ooze her charm all over Steve, she certainly didn't want to hear that, either.

What hurt the most was the idea that he had been going to kiss her. Or maybe that wasn't what hurt the most. Maybe the real pain came from her wounded pride because, deep down, she knew she'd wanted him to, that she would have let him, and that she had been disappointed when her sister had come into the room.

Now she was glad. Michelle's ill-timed entrance had momentarily irritated Janet. Now she saw it as a relief, a blessing that had kept her from making an even bigger fool of herself.

She buried her face in the pillow after flinging herself on the bed. It was dark against the soft surface—enough, she hoped, to blot out all unpleasantness. However, even in the darkness she kept seeing Michelle's black hair and Steve's brown hair so close together while they discussed Janet. Oh, she could just hear them.

"I can't imagine what's gotten into Janet," one would say.

The other would reply, "You'd think she'd be old enough not to be going through so much adolescent turmoil. Maturity seems to come hard for poor Janet."

And all the while they were discussing her, their minds would really be on each other. Michelle would be doing her best to get the message across in a subtle way that she wanted him back and Steve would be wondering if he was really receiving the right message . . . did he dare make a move . . . did he dare ask her out again.

Janet, of course, couldn't see and hear a thing from the other room. Her imaginings, however, were very real and very painful. Until this moment she had not, perhaps, realized just how badly she had wanted to believe that Steve cared for her as much as she did for him and that Michelle no longer mattered to him. Only now did she realize how much it would have meant to her if she had been able to say casually,

"Steve, I think Michelle likes you. I think she wants to go out with you again, that she's sorry she ever let you go in the first place," and to have Steve laugh and say, "You gotta be kidding. Michelle's nothing to me. I have the girl I want. *You.*"

The imaginary words floated in Janet's head. There was no chance that would ever happen. She had told herself that Steve was different, that he was funny and kind and had the same wild sense of humor she did. She thought of their daisy game and the penguin walk and the way he had asked that poor waitress to judge their red nose contest. While she thought about those things, tears filled her eyes. They made her furious. Janet Lindquist did not cry over boys. As mad and as hurt as she had been, she hadn't cried over Mark or Johnny because they weren't worth it. Well, Steve Wayman wasn't worth it, either. He was just like all the rest. Not real and warm, just polyester inside. Yet the tears continued to flow. He might not be worth it, but this was one time she could not control her tears.

There was a timid knock on her door. "Janet?" Michelle called. "May I talk to you?"

Janet squeezed her eyes as tightly shut as possible, trying to stop the tears. She swallowed hard, not wanting a quiver in her voice to betray the fact that she had been crying.

"It's okay, Michelle. I'm not mad. I'm all right. But I guess I'm tired. If it's okay with you, let's talk later. If there's really anything to talk about."

Outside the door, there was a pause as Michelle hesitated. "Well, all right. Steve and I are going to take a short ride. We'll be back pretty soon."

"Fine," she managed to reply.

When she was sure Michelle was out of earshot, she let out a groan of frustration and fell back on her bed again. So it had started already. How was she going to handle this? How was she going to act? Not for the first time, Janet felt like an alien in her own home. She couldn't go anywhere else and get away from it all. Long ago, when all this rivalry had first set in, she had been a lot younger. *Then* she had conjured up all sorts of wild schemes for running away from home and getting away to where the prettier and more beloved daughter didn't have a part in her world. *Now* she was mature enough to know that such action wasn't possible for her. Not until after her senior year. *Then* it would be possible. And she wasn't going to waste any time in making the possibility a reality.

For the first time in a long while, she reached in the drawer and pulled out the college brochures. She looked them over to see which ones would accept new students for the winter semester. A few students always started college after only one semester of their senior year. She would have enough credits for a high school diploma by that time. Why stick around Barkley when she could be out and away and getting on with her *real* life?

She stayed shut away in her room until Nancy knocked on the door and called, "Dinner's almost ready, dear. Freshen up and come on out."

Janet thought about saying she wasn't hungry. She gave up on that immediately. Mom would never buy it. With a sigh of resignation, she called back, "Okay. Be there in a few minutes."

As much pain as the thought of Steve and Michelle together gave her, Janet found herself wishing they would stay out long enough so that Michelle would miss dinner. By tomorrow she would be up to acting natural. This evening . . . well, she just wasn't sure. She took off the baggy, splotched sweat pants and the oversized shirt. When they were in a heap at her feet, she gave them a vicious kick until they joined another pile of dirty laundry in the corner of her room.

Janet looked around her and gave a sigh. It didn't bother her, but she knew her room was beginning to look bad. It wouldn't be long before she'd hear those familiar words from her mother, "You need to clean and straighten up your room, Janet. It looks like a pigsty. Why, I'd be ashamed to have anyone look in there. Take care of it right away."

She opened her closet door and looked down at the clutter on the floor. There were things in that heap that had been there for years. That didn't bother her, either. In fact, it was downright comforting to see the mementos of her childhood tangled with her shoes and belts and winter scarves and caps.

From the closet, she selected an oxford shirt and a pair of clean jeans. She even went so far as to tuck the shirt down inside the jeans and put on a belt that matched the shirt. When that was done, she moved into the bathroom quickly and locked the door behind her.

Head held defiantly, she looked at her mirrored image. She was a mess. It was apparent that she had been crying. Her face was pale and wan, her nose red, and her eyes bleary. To top it all off, her hair was a tangled mess from wrestling around with the pillow.

Pride counted for something. And no one—but no one—was going to see her looking like that. Why, they'd either ask a bunch of dumb questions or they would pretend they didn't notice, but she would be able to tell they were feeling sorry for her. Either way would be bad. She didn't intend to put up with it.

For a long, long time, she splashed cold water on her face to take away its blotchy appearance and to make her eyes seem less red. It was too bad, she thought, that there wasn't some way to make her hair less red, too. But she didn't like that idea, either. There was nothing wrong with red hair, for Pete's sake. Nothing at all. What was the matter with her? Hairbrush in hand, she brushed her hair until the tangles had come unsnarled and what remained was a shining mass of red-gold ringlets that fit her head like a cap.

For the first time since she had been thirteen years old and in an experimental stage, she resorted to makeup. Not that she was about to go overboard. But she wanted to make sure no traces of her recent cry showed. Among Michelle's things, she found a compact and ran the puff lightly over her nose and cheeks. That helped. A touch of pale-pink blusher, an even smaller touch of lip gloss, and she was satisfied.

Janet Lindquist looked fine. She looked like a happy, healthy seventeen-year-old girl who didn't have a worry in the world. Reassured by that image, false though it was, Janet went to join the family. Michelle was there. Janet had really supposed she would be. All in all, this hadn't exactly been her lucky day.

"You look nice," Nancy commented.

"Don't sound so surprised," Janet said with a grin. "Not even I can look a mess all the time."

"But you sure give it a good try," Michelle said, then immediately looked guilty. She had apparently made the comment before she'd thought about the earlier stormy episode.

"That's just my image. I have to fight to preserve it," she said brightly. I might look into acting as a career, she thought, because this has to be an Academy Award–winning performance.

During dinner, the conversation was relaxed and happy. Janet seemed to be the only one feeling any stress. She had been prepared to force down enough food to keep her mother from asking questions. To her surprise, however, the plate of meat and vegetables disappeared without difficulty. Her spirits may have been in bad shape but her stomach was definitely empty and appreciated being fed.

"I've been thinking," she said as casually as possible while Nancy passed around dessert plates filled with hot apple pie, "about next year. How would you feel if I started college at midterm instead of waiting until the next fall? I have enough credits and quite a few kids do, you know."

The other three Lindquists all looked at her in surprise—in

fact, they couldn't have looked more startled if she had announced she were going on a safari in Africa.

"Why, I don't know," Roger said slowly. "I just hadn't thought about it. I guess it's up to you. Just make sure you don't jump into something you'll be sorry about."

"I wouldn't do it for anything," Michelle said firmly. "Your senior year is so special. And the last time you'll get to be with the same bunch of people. There are so many activities for seniors at the end of school. It's a lot of fun."

"You would miss out on a lot, dear," Nancy replied anxiously. "Why, you wouldn't even get to go through the graduation ceremony with your class. I know, I know . . . you get your diploma all right. But if you don't attend that last semester, the school doesn't allow you to participate in the ceremony. I know because Peggy Thompson's boy did that last year and I think he was really sorry to miss graduation."

"But all that stuff doesn't mean anything to me, Mom. You know it doesn't."

"Well, just be sure," her father said again. "You don't have to decide right now. Think about it. After all, the decision is yours. Gosh, it's hard to believe that both my girls are so grown-up and nearly ready to leave home."

"Don't go getting sentimental, Dad," Janet said with a grin. "You know you're looking forward to getting us out from under your feet."

"How can you tell?" he said, giving her an answering grin and a special look that told her he didn't really want to get rid of them at all.

"You and Steve have a nice ride uptown?" Janet asked her sister. She was amazed at how natural and easy the question sounded. Just an everyday, run-of-the-mill question.

Michelle shrugged her slender shoulders. "It was okay. We just talked a lot. I think you hurt his feelings a little."

And what did he do to *mine?* Janet fumed inwardly.

"Oh, I doubt that," she said out loud. "If so, I'll

apologize. Like I said, I was just tired. I feel a lot better now."

"You look fine," Michelle said. She put down her fork and gave Janet a long, curious look that Janet could not read. "You really do. That blusher looks good on you. Next time try the coral. I think it'll look better with your coloring."

And that was that. The day had been tumultuous. Inside she was still feeling the aftereffects; externally, however, the day was ending on a very ordinary note. Just another day like any other.

Chapter Eight

On the Sunday before school started again after the holiday break, Janet was in an unusually pensive mood. She wasn't as depressed and tearful as she had been when she'd finally accepted the fact that Steve was still very interested in Michelle. But it was hard to go back to being her former, cheerful self.

Only a few days had lapsed since she had accused Steve of being a polyester person. In those few days, she had done her best to avoid him. What could she possibly say to him? Before that day, conversation between them had been free and easy. And now Janet cringed at the thought of running into him. He would want to know what had brought on her strange behavior. Or, worse yet, he would have guessed what her problem was and would be terribly kind and considerate and not say anything at all. Janet thought that would be worse than questions.

Being basically an honest and courageous person, however, her own behavior began to bother her. She couldn't let the situation go on like this. Steve lived right next door. Avoiding him completely was going to be impossible, especially when he started dating Michelle again. Janet was so certain this event was going to occur that, in her mind, she didn't say *if* but *when*. Besides, since the night of the football homecoming dance Steve and Janet had been practically inseparable. She couldn't just shut Steve out of her life without any kind of an explanation. Maybe some people could, but not Janet.

On Saturday, the temperature had risen sharply and, at last, the ugly mounds of snow were beginning to melt into rivulets of water that flowed across the ground and sidewalks. Janet looked outside and sighed. She was glad the snow and ice were finally disappearing, but it was all still so dreary.

Going to her room, she located her blue quilted jacket beneath a pile of winter garments thrown across the chair. For no particular reason, she opened a drawer and withdrew the necklace Steve had given her for Christmas. At least it hadn't changed. The daisy was on the outside and the miniature white unicorn looked back at her from the inside. Once she had thought the gift had some special meaning. The delicate gold locket rested lightly in her palm and kept any secrets it knew to itself. Perhaps it did have a special meaning. But whatever meaning it had wasn't quite special enough. She wanted the locket to mean "I love you" when it probably meant "You're a good friend."

Janet wasn't knocking friendship. She had some awfully good friends and she hoped to go through life making more. But simple friendship wasn't what she felt for Steve and it wasn't what she wanted from him.

Abruptly, she put the locket back in place and shoved the drawer shut. She zipped the blue jacket all the way up, squared her chin, and thought, It isn't what you want in life that counts—it's what you get.

"I'm going next door for a while," she called to her mother.

Without waiting for a reply, she went out the door. Not

stopping to think, she ran across the muddy lawns instead of taking time to go around by the sidewalks. When her shoes hit the soggy earth, she groaned inwardly. By the time she had crossed both yards and reached the Waymans' door, her new shoes didn't look new any longer. She could just imagine what her mother would say. They had looked so clean—gleaming white with a blue stripe down the sides. Maybe, she mused, the company should come out with a new line in mud-brown for people like herself. Surely she wasn't the only klutz in the world who didn't get along well with white shoes.

She pressed the Waymans' doorbell. While she waited, she continued to look down at the soiled Nikes. Falling into her habit of talking to herself, Janet said, "Mom is going to kill me. I wonder if I can buy a new pair before she finds out."

Looking up, she saw Margaret Wayman standing there. She was looking at Janet with that slightly amused expression she so often had when Janet was around. However, it wasn't an unkind or patronizing look and Janet took no offense.

"It's amazing what soap and water will do, Janet. I wouldn't buy a new pair just yet."

Instead of blushing as she had when she'd first met Steve's parents, Janet laughed. "Caught me talking to myself again, didn't you?"

Margaret smiled slightly. "I can understand why you talk to yourself. You're a very clever girl. I'm sure you have some amusing conversations. Come on in."

Janet regarded the older woman carefully. She wore her graying hair teased and heavily sprayed in a style that hadn't really been popular for years, and she was still wearing double knit. Janet rarely saw her in a garment of any other fabric. She made most of her own clothes and apparently had a passion for the stretchy, easily handled material. This time the outfit consisted of a pair of purple pants and a flowered top. Despite Janet's dislike of polyester and hairspray, however, she liked Mrs. Wayman. She hadn't thought about why. It was just a good feeling that had gradually come to flow between them. The fact that Steve's mother asked her to come in without hesitation even though Janet would ruin her pale carpet only made Janet like her more. With Margaret, people's feelings came first, material objects were secondary. That was an attitude Janet liked, not that she had any intention of going inside. Even if she had been inclined to do so, her own mother would have had a fit.

"Uh, no thanks," she said. "I'm too messy right now. Could you just have Steve come out, please?"

"Well, I would, dear, but he isn't here. He left just a few minutes ago. Shall I have him call you or come over?"

Janet thought her neighbor looked a bit flustered. Maybe it was just her imagination. "It doesn't matter," she said casually. "If you happen to think of it, fine. But don't worry about it. I can't use soap and water. They're leather."

Without blinking an eye, Mrs. Wayman replied, "Wipe off what you can now. When they're dry, knock the rest of the mud off. Then take damp paper towels or an old rag and rub them. With new laces and a coat of white polish, they'll look as good as new."

Janet grinned. "You're getting used to the way I think and talk, aren't you?"

"You bet I am," Steve's mother said, laughing. "I enjoy the challenge. I've never known anyone before who could make such rapid transitions in midconversation. See you later, Janet. Take care."

"You, too."

Janet went home via the sidewalks this time. No point in adding to the damage, she thought. She glanced back at the Waymans' garage. The spot where Steve's Camaro was usually parked was empty. She would have to wait until later to straighten things out.

After leaving her muddy shoes at the door, Janet raced up

to her room, hoping to get her jeans and shoes cleaned up before her mother saw them. She quickly changed from the soiled jeans to clean ones, gathered up her load of dirty clothes, and headed toward the laundry room. For a moment, the silence of the house puzzled her. The door to Michelle's room was open. Janet glanced inside at the spotless blue-and-white room, so neat it was nauseating, and saw that her sister wasn't there. As she passed by the living room, she looked in to see her father stretched out in his recliner. The newspaper had fallen across his chest and he was sound asleep. Michelle wasn't in there, either, yet she had seen her car on the street.

Janet grabbed her muddy shoes and ran down to the basement. After putting the clothes into the washing machine, she spread out old newspapers on the floor and vigorously attacked the job of cleaning up her shoes. While she scrubbed and scraped, her mind was in a busy whirl. Steve wasn't home. His mother had looked worried when Janet asked for him. Michelle wasn't home, and only Steve's car was missing. To Janet, that meant only one thing: Steve and Michelle were off together giggling and having fun. Maybe they were even holding hands. The only time Steve had ever held Janet's hand was when he'd tried to keep her from falling down when they'd walked in the snow and ice. It just wasn't fair. Michelle could have had any guy she wanted. Why did she have to pick Steve?

When all the mud was removed from her shoes, she sat them on top of the clothes dryer to dry. Tilting her head, she studied them. If she could manage to polish the white part without getting any polish on the blue stripe, they just might look okay. When that was done, she walked back into the kitchen and grabbed her jacket.

"Uh, Mom, I'm going to go out for a few minutes. I won't be long. Does it matter which car I take?"

Nancy shook her head in an absentminded way, then opened the oven door to pull out a pan of perfect, golden-brown tart shells, and slide in another pan of unbaked ones.

Just as Janet was leaving, her mother called, "Janet, where are you going?"

Wearily, Janet shut the door and turned around to face her mother. Couldn't she go out for even a second without having to explain her every move? In truth, she didn't know where she was going. She just felt the urge to drive around for a few minutes. She did some of her best thinking when driving.

Without waiting for her answer, however, Nancy grabbed for her purse and pulled out her wallet. "If you don't mind," she said, "would you stop at a grocery store and get me another packet of frozen fruit? I seem to have extra crusts made up, so I might as well fill them. That way we can have plenty for my bridge club and for dessert tonight."

Janet breathed a sigh of relief. She wasn't being given the third degree, merely being asked to run an errand.

"Sure thing, Mom. Cherries, blueberries . . . what kind do you want?"

Nancy handed her the money and said, "Get whatever you want, dear. I'm making cherry for tomorrow, but if you want a different flavor, that's fine."

Janet nodded, then went out to the garage, got into her father's car, and backed it out. She rode around and tried to think. She thought about going to see Kay, but she lived several miles out and Janet had said she wouldn't be gone long. She thought about Melissa and rejected the idea. There wasn't anything wrong with Melissa, but Janet felt like she wouldn't be good company and Melissa always counted on her to be funny and clever.

When Janet had left, she'd had no specific destination in mind. Yet as she steered the car around the familiar streets, she knew what she was looking for. And she found it. Steve's Camaro was parked at Wendy's. Two familiar-looking profiles shared a corner table. Not that she had really doubted they were together. She'd known all along.

She drove around alone for a while longer. There was a

funny sort of feeling inside her. At first, she didn't recognize the feeling. Then she remembered it was a lot like the way she had felt when she was ten years old and had looked for her dog, Moochie, for two days. With all her heart, she had hoped and hoped she would find her little dog. When a lady on Ninth Street had told her that a dog answering his description had been hit by a car and killed in front of her house, Janet had realized Moochie was really gone for good. And that was the best way she could think of to describe how she felt now. Caring for Steve as she did, it seemed only natural that she should want him to care about her in the same way. Well, he didn't. She had finally gotten that through her thick skull and she knew now that Steve was gone for good.

Chapter Nine

"Hey, something smells great in here," said Steve.

When he and Michelle had gotten home, Michelle had gone promptly to her room. Probably to comb her already perfectly arranged hair, Janet had thought meanly. Steve had stayed behind in the kitchen with Janet and her mother. The room had been spacious enough before, but now it seemed somewhat crowded. His big frame seemed to dwarf everything and everyone about him. In spite of his size, however, he looked about five years old as he hungrily eyed the luscious tarts that filled the counter.

"You may drool over the blueberry ones," Janet said in a voice so calm and mild it surprised her, "but the cherry tarts are off limits."

"How come?" he asked indignantly. "Cherry's my favorite."

"The cherry's for my mom's bridge club," Janet explained. "The blueberry's for home."

"You could have checked with me first before you decided which flavor to put in our dessert."

Janet gave him an exasperated look. "What do you mean, 'our dessert'? Maybe I'm wrong, but I thought you lived next door. *I* don't come over there and pick out *your* desserts."

"Wish you would," he said with a sigh. "My mother means well, but we have some awfully strange desserts."

Knowing Margaret's penchant for the traditional, Janet doubted that. In fact, she knew it wasn't true. She had been around the Wayman house enough to know that dessert was usually chocolate cake or apple pie. However, she was willing to play along.

"I know what you mean," she said. Continuing to set the table, she said no more.

Steve looked at her expectantly. She gave him one of her pseudoangelic smiles.

"Before I finish setting the table, may I ask if you're staying for dinner?"

"Gosh, I don't know. Am I, Mrs. Lindquist?"

Nancy gave him a smile that, unlike Janet's, was warm and real. Janet knew that both her parents adored Steve and made sure he always felt welcome in their home. Since Steve wasn't exactly bashful, they didn't have to work too hard at making him feel at ease. With a twinge of envy, Janet decided that people like Steve and Michelle must be born "at ease." She imagined them making their entry into the world with style and grace, bestowing sweet smiles on the doctors and nurses, instead of bellowing as Janet had. Roger had once laughingly told Janet that the doctor hadn't had to smack her on the bottom, that she had beaten him to the punch by kicking and hollering the moment she was born. "And you haven't changed a bit," he had said, ruffling her curly hair affectionately with his big hand.

Once that story had amused her. Thinking about it now, though, she wasn't amused. From now on, she was going to change. Calmness was going to be her policy.

". . . but you should check with your mother first, Steve. She might have something planned for you."

The last few words of Nancy's reply to Steve entered Janet's consciousness and brought her back to reality. Steve promptly walked toward the phone on the kitchen wall and, in a few moments, received permission to join the Lindquists for dinner.

"How about that, Munchkin?" Steve said, twinkling down at her, then reaching out to tumble her hair in much the same way her father did.

Considering Janet's general mood, the act was a great irritant. Determined to be calm and rational, however, she continued to smile. Until now, it had never occurred to her what a difficult feat smiling was when you had to do it against your will.

"This is your lucky day, Lindquist," he continued. "You get me *and* blueberry tarts for dinner."

"If I got any luckier, I don't think I could stand it," she retorted.

"You don't sound thrilled," Steve remarked, doing his best to look wounded and hurt.

Struggling to seem indifferent, she shrugged. "I know you're not staying for me. You're staying for the tarts." And for Michelle, she added silently. "Besides," she continued, "I thought you didn't like blueberry—just cherry."

"I didn't say I didn't like blueberry. I just said cherry was my favorite."

"Really, Steve," Nancy said, "it doesn't matter which I serve tomorrow. In fact, a mixture might be a good idea. Why don't I put some of both out for dinner, then I'll have some of both for tomorrow?"

"Ah, gee, that's nice, but you don't need to do that for me. Blueberry's fine. It really is."

"Nonsense, Stephen. If you like cherry better, then you shall have cherry."

With that, she briskly transferred a mixture of tarts to a serving plate, then put the rest away in covered containers for the women who would descend upon the Lindquist household tomorrow. Janet was glad she wasn't going to be here. School sounded good compared to a bunch of ladies who seemed to have one big thing in common: a desire for one-upmanship.

"But that really doesn't sound right," she said aloud. "I'm not in favor of changing the entire English language but it is true that some words don't work."

The expressions Nancy and Steve wore were identical as they regarded the red-haired, brown-eyed girl with blueberry filling on the tip of her nose. She was wearing very faded jeans and a sweat shirt Kay had given her. It bore the name of some obscure out-of-state college Kay's brother had attended for a semester. Whether he had abandoned the school or it had abandoned him had never been made clear. Knowing Howard as she did, Janet had always suspected the move had been the school's idea. But at least she had gotten a free sweat shirt out of the deal.

"Why's everyone looking at me?" she asked. "Oh, I know, I bet I have blueberry on my face."

"You *always* have something on your face," Steve said affectionately. "The first time I met you, you were all dressed up but you had cheese on your throat."

Janet remembered that little incident all too well. "The throat isn't on the face," she said for the sake of argument.

"But it's in the general vicinity. However, what your mother and I are wondering is what you're talking about. You know, the bit about some words not working."

"Oh, that," she replied airily. "I was thinking about one-upmanship and how a lot of women practice it but it doesn't sound right to say one-upwomanship."

"Hmmmm. You've got a point. Even one-uppeopleship doesn't have a good ring to it."

Nancy shook her head and withdrew the steaming casserole from the oven. "Janet, I'll never understand you."

This time, however, the words were spoken kindly and had no sting.

"Want to know what we were having for dessert at home, Janet?"

"Not particularly."

Pretending he didn't hear, he continued, "Gooseberry pudding."

"Gooseberry pudding?" she commented. "Likely story. I'd place my money on either chocolate cake or apple pie."

"Then you'd lose," he said solemnly. "Mom distinctly said, 'I made gooseberry pudding with a polyester sauce. I'll save you some for a bedtime snack.' "

Janet laughed in spite of herself. "What's with you this evening, Steve? You seem determined to bring up everything I did wrong the first time we met."

He smiled a strange sort of smile that could have meant anything . . . or nothing.

"I dunno. For some reason, I've been thinking about that today. Maybe I've been thinking about it ever since you called me a polyester person the other day."

Nancy shot Janet a questioning look. Janet acted as if she didn't notice, but she felt a flush steal over her face. She was beginning to wish she were somewhere else.

"Am I supposed to be understanding this conversation?" Nancy asked, pausing in her dinner preparations.

"Not particularly," Janet answered quickly. "It's sort of like one of those inside jokes. You know, where you had to be there to understand. It wouldn't seem funny if I explained."

Since she had finished her tasks, she decided to leave the kitchen to get away from Steve. Steve, however, followed blithely behind her.

"Was that what it was . . . a joke?" he asked. "That bit about me being a polyester person."

His tone was light. His eyes told her his question was more serious than he was willing to let on.

"Sure," she replied casually. Never again was she going to get involved in a serious conversation with Steve. "What else? You know me, Steve. The original laugh-a-minute girl."

"Great. That's what I thought. Just checking to be sure. When a guy's insulted, he needs to know whether to be offended or to laugh."

"Laugh. Definitely laugh. There's absolutely no future in anything else."

"Life does have its serious side," he stated, looking down at her in a way that made her wish more than ever he'd go away completely. Even knowing that he liked Michelle, he had this weird ability to make her feel like Jell-O inside: shaky and wobbly. She mentally envisioned her entire digestive tract shaking and shimmying around. The image brought something else to mind and she hummed a little tune.

Steve looked at her closely. There was a curious smile on his face that resembled tenderness. She didn't need that, either. Not right now.

"What are you humming? And why?" he asked.

Flushing slightly, Janet replied, "Oh, it's just a real old song I heard once on some TV show."

"And?"

"You wouldn't know it."

"Give me a try."

He stood there in the hallway, not allowing her to escape as she so badly wanted to do.

"It's called 'Shimmy Like My Sister Kate,' " she said, feeling like a total idiot. "It's an old song from the Roaring Twenties."

"I see," he said gravely.

"I told you you'd never heard of it."

"Oh, I've heard of it. It's a flapper thing or something. But I'm wondering why it flashed into your mind when you were supposed to be thinking about the serious side of life."

Janet shook her head vigorously, red curls flying. "It isn't worth looking for, Stephen. Hunting for it is only asking for trouble."

After another long, contemplative look, he shrugged. "You wish you could shimmy like your sister Kate? Can't you? Ever do the Charleston, Janet?"

"Once," she admitted, then laughed as the memory came flooding back. "When Mom still had hopes I'd be a lady, she had me take dancing lessons. I think I was about eight years old when we had a recital, and along with several other kids I had to wear a flapper outfit and do the Charleston to some song from the twenties. It was fun. I liked doing *that* a lot better than ballet or tap. Only I got to showing off during the actual performance and got so involved with the part where you work your hands and knees to make it look like your knees are crossing that I lost my balance and fell. Right in the middle of the stage. The audience roared. Mrs. Gabel was furious because I had ad-libbed. Daddy thought it was funny. Mom tried to be nice but she was mortified and never made me take another lesson."

"So you've always been like this," he commented with a grin.

"More or less. And it threatens to go on forever."

"Good. I'd hate to see you change."

"Why?"

He made a funny face at her. "Because you're you. Special. Different. Unique. I've never known anyone quite like you."

"That can be taken two ways, you know."

"So can being called a polyester person," he reminded gently.

"Look, will you drop that bit? I'm sick of the polyester subject."

"Okay. If I'm anything, I'm agreeable. Let's dance."

Janet stared at him as if he had lost his mind. She wasn't too sure he hadn't.

"*Dance?* Right here and now? In the hallway with no music and dinner ready at any minute?"

"Why not? I can't wait another second to see you do the Charleston."

She gave a deep sigh. If she did the Charleston, she would look like a fool. After a moment of reflection, she decided that wasn't a big problem since that was how she had spent the majority of her life. So she grinned at Steve, her brown eyes beginning to sparkle impishly, and began singing the silly song. When she hit a spot where she didn't know the words, she hummed. She started the steps and movements remembered from that childhood dance class. Soon Steve joined in with her and, right there in the middle of the hall, they rolled their eyes, kicked up their heels, and crossed their palms across their knees.

Janet started giggling. Once she started, she couldn't stop. Soon the giggling advanced to such a degree that it was impossible to continue dancing.

"Hey, don't quit now," Steve protested. "I'm just beginning to get the hang of it."

"I can't," she said, holding on to her sides. "My stomach hurts, I laughed so much."

"Say, you two are pretty good," commented Roger from the doorway. He was standing there watching them, Michelle at his side. She looked as beautiful as ever in her bright-red sweater with her makeup perfect and her hair brushed to a high sheen.

"You *are* good," Michelle said.

Janet looked at her in surprise.

"Really," her sister continued. "Even without music, you looked good. Polish it up a bit, get the right costumes, and that would make a terrific number for the variety show. We need acts. Not many have signed up so far."

Janet shook her head. "Not me. No way. In the hall, that's one thing. Before the student body of Barkley High, that's something else. I'd fall like I did in that recital years ago."

Michelle, a member of the student council which was sponsoring the variety show, wasn't about to give up easily. "Well, think about it. All we seem to get are kids who want to pantomime records and girls who do gymnastics. A lively twenty-three-skiddoo act . . . that'd be something different. See if you can talk her into it, Steve."

"I'm not Steve," Roger said, "but it sounds like a terrific idea to me. Maybe you'd even have fun, Janet."

"Did you do the Charleston when you were in high school?" Steve asked Roger.

The older man gave him a strange look.

Janet quipped, "Steve, you're just about to lose your status as adopted son around here. Unless he's fibbing about his birthday Dad wasn't even born yet in the twenties, let alone doing the Charleston in a beaver coat. Or whatever it was they wore."

"Sure, sir," Steve said with an easy grin. "I know that. I was just kidding. Gosh, I know how young you are. Bet you barely remember the twist."

"Just barely," Roger replied with a wry expression. "In fact, I think that's what's the matter with my back today. Imitating Chubby Checker was rough on the sacroiliac."

"Dinner's ready," Nancy called from the other room.

Janet wasn't hungry but she was grateful for the interruption. With a little bit of luck, the subject wouldn't arise again. If her parents started pushing and nagging, she was a dead duck. The way she felt about Steve and Michelle right now, about the last thing she needed was to work with them on a cheery little routine for the dumb variety show.

Her luck continued in its usual vein, however. The plates had scarcely been filled when Michelle started in. *This* time she turned those big, beautiful eyes directly on Steve.

"Steve, you never did say what you thought of my idea."

"Oh, I don't know," he mumbled. "I think I'd feel a little silly."

Bravo, Steve, Janet cheered silently.

"What idea is that, dear?" Nancy asked. "I think I missed out on something."

In a quick, breathless voice, Michelle explained about the variety show. Janet observed her sister with a certain cynicism. This wasn't the first time she had noticed that Michelle only used that breathless way of talking when interesting males were present. She probably thought it was sexy or something. Personally, Janet thought it was revolting, but of course, no one asked her opinion on the subject.

"Why, I think that sounds like a cute idea," Nancy said. "What's your objection, Janet?"

Janet tried to smile. It was difficult because her teeth wanted to remain clenched together. "Remember the last time I did the Charleston in public?"

Nancy gave a genuine laugh. Apparently all the years since it had happened had enabled her to view the incident with humor rather than humiliation. "Well, you've grown up a lot since then. Besides, if it's supposed to be a comedy sort of act, it wouldn't hurt if you *did* fall down. I think you should do it, hon."

"It's like I said," Michelle put in eagerly, "we want this to go over big and we're really having a hard time getting people to participate. I'd really appreciate it if you two would—"

Between clenched teeth, Janet told her sister, "If you think it's such a terrific idea, then why don't *you* team up with Steve?"

Michelle sat back in her chair and gave her that wide-eyed, innocent look that drove Janet crazy.

"Why, I can't," Michelle said simply. "You and Steve dance well, but you were doing it in . . . well, kind of an exaggerated way that was wild and truly funny. I can't be funny. I've tried and it just doesn't work. If I did the Charleston with Steve, it would just be the Charleston. With you two, it's fun. It has pizzazz. It's a comedy. I wish I could be funny but . . ."

Poor, poor Michelle. She has everything else in the world going for her and now she's sorry that she isn't a comedienne to boot. How greedy can you get?

Janet narrowed her eyes as she thought. The look she gave her sister wasn't pleasant at all. "I won't do it," she said firmly. Her chin had squared off in that determined, stubborn way it had of doing.

"Steve?" Michelle's eyes were even wider as she looked beseechingly at their neighbor.

"Look," he mumbled, squirming in his chair, "I'll go along with it if the student council really needs us. Guess it won't be the first time I've made a fool of myself. But it's up to Janet. If she doesn't want to, we can't force her."

From across the table, Janet watched Michelle's face. Tears were beginning to fill her eyes and her lower lip quivered.

"Please, Janet. I don't ask many favors. Can't you do just this one thing for me? I'd do it if I could. I'd try real hard to be as funny as you are, but I've already signed up to sing a folk song while Rod Jeffries plays his guitar and no one is allowed to be in more than one act. Please . . . we need your help so much."

And that was that. Michelle was nearly crying, so of course both parents begged until Janet would have felt like a rat if she'd continued to refuse. Although she agreed to at least try a few rehearsals, she was filled to bursting with suppressed hostility.

She supposed she loved her sister. After all, they were in the same family. It sure would be a lot easier, though, Janet thought, to love Michelle if they were separated by a couple of hundred miles. At least. That poor, pitiful act was hard to stomach, but it worked. For Michelle, that is. But Janet didn't like being manipulated by tears and misplaced sympathy. Who cared about a high school variety show?

Janet finished her meal mechanically. She cleared her plate to avoid questions, not because she wanted the food. It went down with difficulty and lay there in her stomach like a rock. Not even the blueberry tart topped with fresh whipped cream held much appeal. As soon as she had forced down the last bite, she asked to be excused.

"Don't you want to try one of the cherry ones?" her mother asked.

Janet's stomach roared and rumbled in protest at the very mention of the idea. "Uh, I don't think so. Maybe later. Right now I have some things I need to do in my room."

"How about some Scrabble when you're done?" Steve asked. He was happily munching his third tart. The events of the evening hadn't damaged his appetite at all.

"I don't think so," she said. "I have way too much to do."

She pushed back her chair, got up, and walked out of the kitchen. When she was almost to the door of her room, she looked back to see Steve following her. She supposed he was trying to be kind to her. She wished he'd give it up. She didn't need kindness from him. Or anything else.

"Hey, kid, before you go do these things that are so pressing and important," he said, "I just wanted to tell you that I hope you don't mind about this variety show thing. It seemed to matter a lot to Michelle and it can't hurt us, can it?"

She looked him squarely in the eye and said, "I never had much desire to be either a rat or a sucker. When it came right down to the wire, I picked sucker. Maybe rat would have been a better choice."

Steve put his hands on her shoulders, squeezed hard, and laughed heartily. He asked no questions about what she meant. That was just the way it was with her and Steve. They *knew* without a lot of explanations of how each other's minds worked. Too bad, she thought wistfully, that this rapport didn't extend beyond friendship.

"Change your mind about a game of Scrabble? Last chance."

She shook her head, this time refusing to meet his eyes. "Not tonight, Steve. Maybe Michelle will, but I just have too much to do. See you later."

"Of course you will. After all, we'll have to practice."

"Practice?"

"Sure. You know, the Charleston."

"Oh, that," she said with a deep sigh of regret. "Don't remind me."

"It could be worse, Janet."

In her most mournful voice, she replied, "I don't see how."

On that note, she opened the door to her room, walked inside, and closed the door.

Chapter Ten

"Janet, you're not even trying to cooperate," Michelle said. She had started out looking exasperated. The more they had practiced, the more that exasperation had turned into despair. In fact, now she appeared close to tears. Maybe even genuine tears, Janet thought.

She knew she wasn't doing well. Perhaps she should feel sorry. She didn't. This *thing* had been thrust upon her against her will and she wanted no part of it. Instead of admitting, however, that there was a problem, she gave an impatient groan and said, "What's wrong this time, Miss Director?" Her tone was openly sarcastic and she didn't even care. Not even when Steve glanced at her in surprise. Just because *he* handled Michelle with kid gloves didn't mean she had to.

"Everything," Michelle said, throwing up her hands in a gesture of frustration. "When I saw you two dancing in the hall that day, I thought it was the cutest thing I'd ever seen. It was lively and funny and wild. And now . . ."

"Yes?" Janet asked, lifting her eyebrows in a way she hoped looked sophisticated and blasé.

"It looks wooden and stiff," Michelle said flatly. "You hate every minute of it and it shows. And how can poor Steve look like he's having fun when you wear that bored expression and move like a puppet on a string?"

"Look, you can cancel the act. It isn't written in blood anywhere that this particular act must go on. Barkley High can survive without it."

The threat of tears passed away from Michelle's face. In its place was a look Janet hadn't seen very often. She knew what it meant, though: anger. Her sister had finally had enough. There was a glint in her eye and a set to her chin that made her look more like Janet than she did at any other time.

"You said you would do it," she said. Her words were carefully measured and slowly spoken. "The programs have already been taken to the printer. The show is scheduled and timed right down to the minute. Dave has the sound track for all recorded music on tape, in order, and ready to go. In other words, it'll mess up the whole show if you back out now."

Janet knew Michelle was not exaggerating. The variety show was only a little over a week away. Changes weren't feasible at this point. Maybe she *was* being deliberately obstinate. Not even she knew for sure. When Dad and Michelle had found them acting silly in the hall that day, the moment had been spontaneous. *This* was planned. It simply wasn't the same, no matter how hard she tried. Every time they practiced, Janet felt more and more resentful. She would watch Michelle and Rod as they practiced their number. Sitting on the high stool, with handsome Rod Jeffries beside her, Michelle could sing "Danny Boy" in a way that caused a lump in the throat just at rehearsal in the gym. Janet could just imagine what it would do to people during the real thing when Michelle was all decked out in that flowing blue-and-white dress Mom was making. The Lindquist sisters would be quite a contrast that night. There would be beautiful Michelle singing the plaintive ballad in her clear, true voice . . . and there would be funny Janet with her flapper dress and a long string of beads, rolling her eyes.

Snapping out of her resentful reverie, Janet gave a sigh of

acceptance and said, "Okay, start the dumb record over. I'll try one more time. If it doesn't work, we'll just have to wait till tomorrow. I'm tired and I have homework."

They went through the whole thing from top to bottom. Their movements were faultless and in perfect harmony with the musical accompaniment, but Janet knew Michelle was correct in her assessment of the performance. It lacked life, vitality. She felt so tired and drained. To look as if she were having fun . . . well, it was too big an act.

"That was better," Michelle said with more politeness than truth.

"It was rotten," Janet admitted flatly. "Maybe we'll have better luck tomorrow."

"Let's all take a ride and go get a Coke somewhere," Steve suggested.

Janet knew he only included her to be nice. So often she wished he'd just quit trying to be nice. She knew what was going on and she could handle it.

"No, thanks," she said lightly. "Like I said, I'm tired and I have homework. But go on. Have fun."

Steve looked at her. His expression was distinctly puzzled. He didn't argue or insist, however.

"Whatever you want," he said. "Coming, Michelle?"

"I guess so. I'll run get my jacket. Why don't you come, too, Janet? A short ride and a Coke won't take that long."

She shook her head and didn't look at either of them. "I have a big test in trig tomorrow. Considering what I did on the last one, I better make this one good."

"Maybe I could help you study," Steve offered eagerly. "I did pretty well in there last year, if I do say so myself."

"That's all right," Janet said firmly. "I can handle it. See you later."

"Okay." He still seemed reluctant to leave. "I would like to talk to you soon. When you can work it into your schedule."

"What's that supposed to mean?"

"You tell me. You're the one who's suddenly too busy for everything."

Janet bent her head and covered her face with her hands.

"Later, Steve. Just take Michelle and go get your Cokes now. The world of trigonometry awaits me."

"I'm sure you'll have a fascinating evening," he said, giving her a wide smile that showed all of his white, even teeth, and didn't really look like a smile at all.

"Did I ever claim to be exciting and fascinating?" she mumbled as she disappeared from his sight.

Steve came around the next day after school. Michelle wasn't there. She had stayed late for a special cheerleading practice.

"Ready to practice the Charleston some more?"

"As ready as I'll ever be," she answered without enthusiasm.

"Janet, I said I wanted to talk to you. Before we start practicing is as good a time as any. What's bothering you these days? You just aren't the same."

"Things change. People change." She kept her voice low and bored. She didn't look at his face. "Maybe I'm maturing. Heaven knows it took long enough."

"You aren't maturing," he said bluntly. "You're souring. There's a difference."

"I don't recall asking your opinion."

"Consider it a bonus. You got it for free. Can't beat that."

She felt her temper rising. "What is it everyone wants out of me, anyway?"

His reply was direct and firm. "I didn't want to get roped into this act, either, but since I did, I plan to do my best. Can you honestly say you're trying? Maybe you don't feel good. Maybe something's bothering you. Janet, we all have troubles from time to time. But this is just an *act*, for Pete's sake. Can't you put on an act . . . be a little silly to give the audience a laugh? You go through the routine like a robot.

And while we're at it, I can't understand why you avoid me so. For a while there, we were the best of friends. Now I think you'd have to be threatened with bodily harm before you'd drive around the block with me to get a soda. What's wrong?"

Janet couldn't believe this conversation. If anyone knew what was wrong, *he* did. Well, if he could put on an innocent act, so could she.

Very sweetly, she said, "Why, I haven't meant to avoid you, Steve. I'm sorry. But doing well in school has become very important to me."

"So important that friends don't count for much?"

She swallowed hard. There was more than a grain of truth in what he said. Since she had stopped running around with Steve so much, she had somehow fallen into the habit of being a loner. She was friendly with Kay and the other girls during school hours, but she hadn't seen much of them otherwise. She didn't want to go to any of the popular hangouts because she was afraid of seeing Steve and Michelle together. For that reason, she had managed to be "busy" when invitations had been extended. Maybe her life had never been the mad social whirl her sister seemed to enjoy so much, but she'd never been a hermit. Until now.

"No comment?" Steve asked.

"Sure friends are important. Maybe I've let things get out of perspective a little. Since I decided that I want to enter college midterm next year, I've felt I had to do my best in school. I guess I've let it crowd out other things."

The explanation she gave was close enough to the truth to keep her conscience clear but far enough away from it to keep her pride intact.

"Does that admission mean we're going to have a good, relaxed practice and that you'll go somewhere with me afterward for a Coke or something?"

Janet felt trapped. If Steve was so bewitched by Michelle, why couldn't he just take her now that she was willing and let it go at that? What compelled him to continue showing an interest in Janet? She didn't want his kindness. Sometimes she felt like screaming at him: Just go away and leave me alone! I have my daisies and unicorns and dreams of how it's going to be for me someday. That's all I need.

She did not, of course, say that. Instead, she shrugged and said, "Let's practice and see how that goes. Then we'll know if we're in any mood for socializing after that."

The practice was better than usual. Maybe they weren't exactly hilarious yet, but they were livelier than they had been during the past few practices. The recorded music was loud and fast. Steve made funny faces at her that caused her to smile whether she wanted to or not. As she gave herself up to the music and the performance, she felt the tension ease slightly.

"We're better," Steve said breathlessly when the record stopped. "I don't know what's made the difference, but we've definitely improved. Too bad Michelle isn't here to see."

Janet slumped down in a chair to rest and didn't say a word. What was there to say? If Steve didn't know why the practice was better, Janet did. It was because Michelle *wasn't* there. In her presence, Janet was tense and, admittedly, resentful. Her sister had appointed herself director, critic, and choreographer. Janet felt stifled when she knew Michelle was watching, ready to criticize every movement.

"We'll rest a minute, then go through it one more time. You do as well this time and I'll get you some cheese nachos to go with your Coke."

"Trying to fatten me up so I can't fit in my flapper dress?"

"Never, but who started the rumor that cheese nachos are fattening? They are definitely low-cal food. I eat them all the time and look how lean and trim I am."

Steve patted his flat middle and Janet sighed.

"It isn't fair that you can eat so much and not gain any weight at all," she remarked pensively, "when all I have to do is breathe the fumes from a Big Mac and I gain five pounds."

"You look all right to me. Have I complained?"

That was another question she didn't intend to answer. No, he hadn't complained. All he had done was reject her in favor of Michelle.

From where she lounged in the chair, she hummed another song that had come to mind.

"Your mind's off the track again," Steve observed. He didn't act as if he really minded.

"How can you tell?"

"Easy. One, you didn't answer my question. Two, you have a spacey look in your eye. And, three, you're humming a song that has nothing to do with our rehearsal *or* with anything else we've been discussing."

"You know that song?" she asked.

He sang a few bars to show that he did. "It's called 'I'm Gonna Be a Wheel Someday.' "

Janet laughed at his slightly off-key rendition of the rock song from the late fifties or early sixties. "I guess you do know that song. When I was little, I used to play Mom's old singles all the time and that was one of them. She had some weird ones. They ranged all the way from 'Short Fat Fanny' to 'It's Now Or Never.' "

"Then why didn't you hum one of them instead of the one you did?"

"What is this, inquisition time?" she asked irritably.

"No, amateur psychology time. I'd like to be able to figure out what makes you tick, how your mind works."

"Don't bother. In fact, I'm not sure my mind does work. But the reason I hummed that song isn't too deep. Maybe it's sort of my theme song."

When she told him that, she wished she hadn't. It was true that she did want to be a "wheel" someday and forget all the hurt that she was feeling now. But she had to keep the part of Janet Lindquist that was serious and vulnerable hidden away.

And hiding it was especially important where Steve was concerned. To him, she was a funny little clown: a short red-haired girl who was always good for a laugh with juggling acts, corny jokes, and happy-go-lucky attitude.

He stood for a moment with his hands in his pockets. He appeared to be searching for the right thing to say. Janet was way ahead of him, for she knew there was no point in mental gropings. There really wasn't anything to say that could make any difference. Only time could make a difference and it seemed to pass so slowly.

"Is it okay if I say I don't understand you?" he asked.

"It's very much okay," she replied, giving him a smile that wavered only slightly. "After all, it isn't really expected of you. I don't even understand myself. Ready to try the Charleston again, Wayman?"

"Ready as I'll ever be."

It was even better than the last time. Her bad mood and pensiveness forgotten, Janet laughed out loud with pleasure and Steve soon joined her. He reached over and started the record a third time. This time they didn't follow the steps they had rehearsed. Janet improvised some wildly improbable steps and Steve mimicked them. When the recording ended again, they collapsed on the floor, both nearly helpless with giggles.

"I think you've earned your nachos, kid," Steve gasped.

"You bet I did. Maybe even a double order. I surely burned off some calories with all that."

"I'd think so," he said with his slow, easy grin fixed on her face. "Let's get going. I'm starved."

As Steve and Janet were getting ready to go, Michelle suddenly appeared.

"Hey, everybody," she said cheerily. "Did I hear food mentioned? I'm starved. What are we having?"

She stood there looking at Steve and Janet with wide, expectant eyes. As usual, she looked close to perfect in her corduroy skirt and ruffly blouse. But then Michelle looked good in anything.

Maybe it was her imagination, but Janet thought Steve looked a little uneasy. He had shoved his hands back in his pockets. "Oh, we were just going out for a little bit. Get some cheese nachos and a soda. No big deal."

"Sounds great to me," Michelle said quickly. "I'm famished. The yearbook committee meeting ran late today and I didn't have time for lunch and this is Mom's day for volunteer work at the hospital so dinner will be late. I'm ready when you two are."

"Well, sure," Steve replied. "I guess we're ready now, aren't we, Janet?"

Janet looked for a moment at Steve. To her, he was the perfect boy. Then she turned and looked at her sister. From a purely objective standpoint, she had to admit Michelle was the perfect girl. So what was Janet Lindquist doing standing around in their way?

"Janet?" Steve urged, glancing at her in a manner that let her know he realized she was off in her own world again. Lately she was beginning to wonder if she would ever learn to stay in the real world.

Bringing herself back to the present, she said, "Uh, well, I feel all sweaty and messy. Let me go comb my hair and put on a different shirt. I'll be right back."

Of course, she had no intention of going with them. She had merely used that as an excuse to give her time to think up something to tell them. She might want to be a big wheel someday. Right now, however, she had no desire to be a fifth wheel.

"And now you're thinking . . . ?"

The twinkle in Steve's blue-gray eyes had increased.

"About unicycles," she replied promptly, then retreated to her room.

As the door closed behind her, she heard Michelle say, "I don't see how you can carry on a conversation with her, Steve. To me, she makes no sense at all."

Not caring what Michelle said or thought about her, Janet closed the door. Just as if she planned to go with them, she changed her shirt and brushed her hair. After that, she stood in front of the mirror and practiced looking sick. Nausea was a good reason not to go eat nachos.

Doing her best to look wan and forlorn, she walked back into the other room. No one mentioned that she didn't look well. Of course, they were too busy looking at each other to look at her, anyway.

"Steve said the practice went great," Michelle said. "Want to run through it for me?"

"No," Janet replied.

Michelle looked hurt. "Why not?"

"Because I'm tired and don't want to. Because I feel sick to my stomach."

"Oh, Janet," Michelle said impatiently, "when are you going to grow up? You've been 'sick to your stomach' whenever you didn't want to do something for as long as I can remember."

"So?"

"So no one believes you when you say you're sick to your stomach."

Janet was in no mood to be crossed. She glared at her sister. "In the old story about the boy who cried wolf, he *did* get eaten by a wolf. And I *can* get sick."

"Come off it and be honest. You just don't want to do it for me. Isn't that right?"

Michelle's attitude was quickly making Janet angry. She could feel her blood pressure rising.

"Yes, that's right. Just because you're on the dumb student council doesn't give you the right to direct every move Steve and I make on this number. You've appointed yourself boss over the act and we're perfectly capable of doing it without a boss. Namely, without *you*."

"I was only trying to help."

"Then if you want to help, butt out. If I'm going to do this stupid act, then I have to do it my way. Not yours. You butt out or I bow out. Is that clear?"

"Perfectly clear," Michelle replied icily. "But if you fall flat on your rear end again, don't blame me."

"If I fall flat, I'll be expecting to see you leading the cheering section. You don't think I can do anything right, do you?"

"Of course I do. That doesn't have anything to do with this. You're acting like a baby."

Steve looked from one sister to the other. At first he looked almost stunned, then he stepped in and said, "Hey, I think you're both just tired and hungry. Let's go get our snack and forget all this. We'll feel better with some food in our stomachs."

Janet turned and gave Steve a cold and stony stare. "Who appointed *you* to the peace council? Try the UN. They don't seem to be doing so hot."

"Janet, knock it off," he warned. "Let's just go get the nachos and—"

"Steve Wayman, you take those nachos and—"

"Janet!" exclaimed Michelle.

Janet smiled sweetly and said, "I was simply going to say 'and enjoy them to the last bite!' See you around, Ken and Barbie."

With that, she went quickly back to her room. They called to her through the door a few times. She didn't reply. After a while, it was very quiet in the house. Too quiet. Janet knew she was all alone. And that was fine with her. Just the way she wanted it.

Chapter Eleven

"Mom, you're going to *have* to do something about her. She's getting more unbearable by the minute. I never know what she's going to say or do next, except that it will be something rude, sarcastic, or obnoxious."

Janet hadn't meant to eavesdrop. She'd been on her way to the living room when she'd heard Michelle's voice. And Michelle wasn't exactly whispering. Her complaints carried well through the quiet house. Each word was crystal clear.

She could even hear her mother's somewhat impatient sigh.

"I really don't know what you expect me to do, Michelle," Nancy said. "I know Janet's been a bit unpredictable lately. . . ."

"Unpredictable?" Michelle exclaimed. "She's always been unpredictable. What she is now is impossible."

"All right, all right. She *has* been stormier than usual, but I'm sure it's just a phase she's going through. I know Janet well enough to know that asking her what's wrong won't help. When she's ready to confide, she will. Until then, I simply don't know what to do except wait."

Michelle's voice started up again. Instead of going on into the room as she had intended to do, Janet turned and walked back the other way. Let them talk each other's ears off about her stormy, unpredictable, rude, obnoxious, sarcastic behavior, if that was how they enjoyed spending their evenings. She had better things to do than stand around listening.

It made her mad to hear Michelle whining to Mom like that. Her mother's attitude didn't exactly make her feel great, either. She had just sat there and calmly agreed that Janet was an impossible mess but she didn't know what to do about it. There were three other people in this family and not one of them understood Janet. There probably wasn't anyone in Barkley who understood her.

Janet grabbed her coat and headed toward the back door. Roger was in the kitchen making coffee. When he saw Janet moving at lightning speed he looked at her curiously and said, "Where are you going in such a hurry?"

"Just out," she said shortly.

He gave her a reproving look. "That isn't much of an answer. It's late and very cold out. And it's a week night besides. Does your mother know you're leaving?"

"No. And I seriously doubt that she cares. In fact, I think having me out of the house will be a welcome relief to all."

With that, she threw open the door and was greeted by the cold night air.

"Just a minute, young lady. You can't go running off like this without an explanation. Your sister never leaves without giving us details and—"

"And I'm not my sister! I'll be back when I'm back." She gave the door a hard slam and winced at the loud sound it made. She didn't dare take one of the cars. If she did, one of them would drive the other and track her down. Besides, she didn't have her driver's license with her.

She couldn't believe what she had just done: talked back to her father, then run out into the night. Her legs carried her swiftly across the backyard, then on across the neighbors' yards. Once she heard her father call her name. She didn't hear him again after that, whether because he gave up or she was too far away to hear, she didn't know.

Being out here was dumb. The sky was pitch-black. No stars were out and the moon was a thin sliver that gave off very little light. Tears filled her eyes and she hated the feeling of them. They overflowed and cascaded down her face; she hated the salty taste of them as they passed over her lips. Tears were for weak-willed, self-pitying people. Janet Lindquist had little patience with tears. Okay, so she had made a fool of herself and run out of the house. Sooner or later she would have to go back. Everyone there would be angry, worried, irritated . . . all those things she didn't want to cope with right now.

She was honest enough to admit she had brought the whole thing on herself. Once she'd had it all planned out, neatly and smoothly. Her life had been filled with constant daydreams of how it would be when she didn't have to live under her sister's shadow. That was before Steve Wayman had appeared on the scene and managed to win a special place in her heart. The waiting wasn't bearable any longer. She needed to get out now. The trouble was, she was losing her optimism. If no one in her own family liked and understood her, if no one in her entire hometown had any real rapport with her, then what basis did she have for thinking it would be any different when she left Barkley behind? Maybe there *weren't* any kindred spirits out there for Janet Lindquist. Steve had once said she was unique. Maybe she was. But being unique was pretty lonely.

With no particular plan in mind, she kept walking across the yards. A dog barked and lunged at her. Her heart was suddenly in her throat. Even when she realized the dog was chained to its house and couldn't reach her, her pulse continued to race wildly. After that episode, she crossed the front lawn until she hit the sidewalk. Walking alone at night wasn't a very smart thing for a young girl to do, not even in a relatively small town like Barkley. The rational, intelligent part of Janet knew that and she felt safer now that she was under the bright glow of the streetlights. But if the rational part of Janet had been in control, she would have turned around and gone back home to face the inevitable lectures and get it over with. As it was, the angry and resentful part of her was still dominating her actions and her legs kept up their swift movements away from the place that was home.

Confused, unhappy thoughts kept crowding up against her. They pushed out all sense of time and place. On and on she ran, not knowing where her feet were taking her . . . and not caring. It was good to run, to feel the cold wind against her face. If she ran hard enough and fast enough, maybe she could get rid of the bad feelings.

Suddenly Janet was brought abruptly back to reality by the sound of footsteps behind her. Whoever it was back there was running as fast as she was. She speeded up. So did whoever was following her. Soon she was running so hard her sides were aching with the effort. She couldn't keep it up much longer. The other footsteps grew louder, closer. She was losing ground. When the dog had barked and lunged, she had been scared. Now she was terrified.

"Janet! Wait. Will you stop? Jan-et! Please."

She was so relieved to hear the familiar voice she momentarily forgot her anger. Stopping, she turned around to greet Steve.

"Well, Steve, fancy meeting you here."

He was huffing and puffing so that he couldn't reply immediately. They were standing directly under a streetlight. It shed a bright light down on them, the artificial glow giving Steve's handsome, regular features a harsh look. Perhaps he wasn't as angry and upset as he looked. Maybe it was just the weird lighting that made him look that way.

"You're an idiot, Janet Lindquist," he said between gasps.

"You say the nicest things. You went to all this trouble just to tell me that? You shouldn't have bothered."

"You think I wanted to? I was knee-deep in calculus when Michelle called me practically in hysterics. Your dad's out in the car looking for you. I decided to take off on foot. Knowing you, I figured you'd take off down paths he couldn't get the car through."

"And so you found me first. What do you win? A week in the Bahamas? A free order of fries at McDonald's? Don't get your hopes up. I don't think any rewards are going to be offered for my return."

"Should there be?" he asked. His face was still grim and unsmiling. "I imagine *you're* the one who has something coming. And I don't think it's going to be a reward. Lately you've been a real pain."

"Stop it, Steve. I don't care what you think about me or about anything else. Michelle asked you to look for me and, like a good little Boy Scout, you did what she asked. And you were successful. You found me. Consider that your good deed for the day and trot on home to report in. I can take care of myself."

"I don't know what's gotten into you, Janet Lindquist, and right now you've got me so mad that I'm not sure I care what your problem is. All I know is that, like it or not, you're not getting out of my sight this evening. I left a warm house and work I need to be doing to run down dark streets and back alleys looking for you."

"How noble—" she began sarcastically, when Steve suddenly grabbed her wrists and held on with a grip of iron.

In a tone that left no room for argument, he said, "No more talk. Our families are worried and you're too overwrought to make sense. Now, turn around and walk. And I'll be with you every step of the way. You have no choice."

She made one last futile attempt at defiance and independence. "You're not my boss. You have no authority over me. You can't make me do anything I don't want to do."

Still holding her in a firm grip, he looked down at her and

shook his head. His expression said he couldn't believe she was actually talking like that. However, his manner was gentler when he replied, "If you're going to act and talk like a spoiled brat, then expect to be treated like one. Now, let's go home."

He released his hold on one wrist and placed that hand lightly at the nape of her neck. As he moved forward, he retained her right hand in his left one. Janet did walk but she angrily tried to pull her hand from his grasp. The effort was futile.

They walked briskly and silently. Janet now felt the cold as she hadn't felt it when she was running in the other direction. Along with the physical discomfort, she felt a multitude of emotional discomforts. First of all, there was anger: at herself, at Steve, at her parents, at Michelle . . . . and at life in general. Along with the anger, there was a vague sense of disgrace. She had behaved in a childish and foolish way and there was no way she was going to get out of this situation gracefully.

To passersby who didn't look too closely, Janet and Steve appeared to be a typical teenage couple walking along hand in hand. A glance at the pair of grim, unhappy faces would quickly dispel that impression.

It was a long, long walk back home. Janet had gone a lot farther than she'd realized. Not a word was spoken until they were, at last, within a block of home.

"Still mad?" he asked.

"Yes."

"Well, no matter. If you don't feel like thanking me now, you can do it later. No hurry."

"Thank you? Why on earth should I thank you? I didn't ask you to do anything for me and I certainly don't like your overbearing, heavy-handed manner. I guess it's all in keeping with your masculine image."

"It's all in keeping with making sure you stay out of trouble, though I'm beginning to believe that's an impossible task. Look, kid, I know you're in no mood for advice—"

"But you're giving it, anyway, I gather."

"Right," Steve said firmly. Her hand was still locked in his. She had given up the struggle to free it several blocks ago. As angry as she was, she silently admitted a certain grudging thankfulness for the touch of another human being. The trip back home was inevitable. It would have been much longer and scarier alone.

"If you know what's good for you, Janet, you'll go in that house and you'll apologize nicely. Whether you're sorry or not, you'd better act like you are."

"I'm not much on being a hypocrite," she said stiffly.

He shrugged. "Suit yourself. I suppose you will anyway. But, believe me, you'll end up being sorry sooner or later. For the trouble you've caused yourself, if not for what you've put them through. You might as well say it now and get it over with. Less hassle in the long run."

"Boy Scout, bully, philosopher, and Dear Abby all rolled into one."

"Yeah, well, go on and call me what you want. I thought we were friends. I guess I thought wrong."

He stopped walking. She wondered why and looked up at him bewilderedly.

"You're home, Janet," Steve said softly.

Feeling more like an idiot than ever, Janet turned her gaze toward the sidewalk that led up to her house.

"You don't have to come with me," she said, jerking her hand again.

"I'm coming in. I won't stay. But I'm not letting go of you until you're inside that door."

"That's dumb."

"This whole thing's been dumb. You're just trying to stall. Move. . . ."

Resentment flared, then faded as quickly as it had come. Janet's legs felt numb and stiff as Steve steered her toward the entrance of the house. As they approached the front door, all the fight drained out of her. Seeming to sense that, Steve let go of her hand.

"Steve, I'm afraid to go in." Her voice suddenly sounded very small.

He put an arm around her shoulder. It felt warm, supportive, and reassuring.

"I guess, in your place, I'd be scared, too. But it has to be done."

"I know."

Reaching out, she took hold of the doorknob. Before she had gathered up enough courage to turn it, the door flew open and she was face-to-face with her parents. Michelle stood in the background. Her pretty face was pale and drawn.

No one spoke for what seemed like a very long time. It was Steve who finally broke the strained silence. He cleared his throat and said, "Well, I found her."

"So I see," remarked Roger. "Thank you, Steve. I just got back home. Janet, what do you have to say for yourself?"

Actually, she didn't know what she had to say for herself. All she knew was that she felt like she had when she was four years old and had colored pretty pictures all over the living room walls. The deed had been done. Did the reasons matter?

"Can Steve go home first?" she asked softly. "Michelle's already taken him away from homework he needs to be doing. I can't see any reason for him to stand around here and listen to a family fight."

Her father's features were as firmly set as granite. Her mother had obviously been crying—and was ready to start again at any moment. When Roger spoke, it was with careful control. "Of course Steve may go home. You might have manners enough to thank him."

"Why?" she dared to ask. "He didn't do it for me. Good night, Steve."

"Uh, well . . . good night, everyone. Hope it all works out okay. See you after school tomorrow, Janet?"

"Whatever for?" After this evening, she couldn't imagine

why he would ever want to see her again.

"Practice. The variety show's only a few days off. We need all the practice we can get."

"Oh, that. I wish . . ."

"But we can't," he said, anticipating her words as he so often did. "A commitment is a commitment."

Somehow the good-nights all got said. Janet's parents and Michelle thanked Steve profusely even if Janet saw no need to.

"You're determined to add fuel to the fire, aren't you, young lady?" Roger asked grimly.

It wasn't the sort of question that seemed to require an answer. Janet stood there, head down, and waited for the rest of it.

"On top of everything else," he continued, "you were terribly rude to Steve. What was that comment supposed to mean about not doing this for you? Who else did he do it for? *You* were the one out there alone after dark."

"The only reason he came after me was because Michelle asked him to. He did it for her, not for me. She has him twisted around her little finger just like she has all the guys."

"Janet, I think you've got this all wrong," Michelle said.

"Do I?" Janet cried from the depths of her bitterness. "I'm a junior in high school, Michelle, and I've only dated two boys. And those two only asked me out because they were hoping it would help them get closer to you. I'm not saying that's your fault. You're pretty, smart, poised, popular, outgoing—all the things I'm not and never will be. But couldn't you have left Steve Wayman alone the second time around? Surely you could tell how much I liked him, how much I was hoping he'd like me back. But, no, after Jordan went back to college, you had to start in on Steve again. No guy in his right mind is going to ask *me* out when he can have *you*. I hate school. I hate this town. I hate being Michelle Lindquist's klutzy little sister and having everyone feel sorry for me because I don't quite measure up. I can't wait to get away from here so no one can compare me with you."

Michelle had looked pale when Janet first came in; now her face was completely white. "You sound like you hate me." She sounded surprised and hurt.

"Maybe I do," Janet said with complete honesty. "I don't want to. I've tried not to. But I get so sick of being the ugly duckling in the family. I love Steve. I love him so much and—"

"But you've been telling us all he's just your friend," her mother reminded her gently.

"And I guess I was lying to myself more than I was to you. Maybe I thought if I said it often enough, it would be true. Only it didn't work that way. I'd have settled for being his friend if that's all I could have had, but you don't know how hard it is to wonder if he is even my friend or if he just hangs around hoping Michelle will take him back. When they started going out again, I tried not to care. I tried not to let it hurt but it did. It hurts so bad I wish I were dead."

The words were out. All sternness was gone from Roger Lindquist's face. He held out his arms and Janet found herself sobbing against his broad chest. When she was able to quit crying at last, he handed her his handkerchief, again making her feel about four years old. She looked across the room. Michelle and Nancy sat side by side on the couch. They both looked tired and miserable and not too far from tears themselves.

"I'm not going out with Steve," Michelle said. Her voice sounded shaky.

"But you have," Janet insisted. "I've seen you. I know."

"Come sit down with us and talk calmly, hon. I think there's been a big misunderstanding," Nancy said softly.

"I don't want to talk. I just want to go to bed."

"Please, Janet," her father said. "Just for a little while."

Janet sat down on the couch. Her mother reached out to put an arm around her but Janet resisted. Instead, she huddled at the end, knees drawn up under her chin and arms clasped tightly around them.

"Your feeling for Steve has never been a secret, Janet," her mother told her. "It's written all over your face."

"But Michelle went after him anyway. But I suppose that doesn't matter. He never did get over her. Maybe he didn't mean to use me. Maybe he does really like me for a friend but I wanted more and—"

"Michelle hasn't 'gone after' Steve, Janet."

"I knew you'd stick up for her. You always do. She's everyone's pet. Everyone's idea of Miss Perfect."

"That's enough," her father said firmly. "Talk rationally and quit attacking your sister before you know the facts. She said she hasn't been going out with Steve. Do you think she's lying to you?"

Janet blinked and gave the matter some thought. She looked over at her sister. She'd never known Michelle to be dishonest before this.

"But you and he . . . I mean, I saw . . . I . . ."

Michelle's expression was unreadable. Her voice was wooden. "We went some places together. He had some problems he wanted to discuss. But they weren't 'dates.' He hasn't asked me out or shown any signs that he wanted to. Not for a long, long time. And, whether you believe me or not, I wouldn't have gone if he had asked."

Janet recognized the truth of the words. Feeling drained and exhausted, she didn't know what to say.

"Then I guess I've been more of a fool than usual," she said after a pause. "I'm sorry I ran off and acted like such a baby. It won't happen again."

"It was foolish," her dad said gently. "Foolish and dangerous. But I guess you've been having a harder time than any of us realized. Let's just forget about it and try to start all over. Okay?"

Janet nodded silently.

"But one more thing," he said as the four of them stood up to go get ready for bed. "You are *not* a second-class person in this family or in this community. And you're definitely not an ugly duckling. It's true that you and your sister aren't much alike. You both have good and bad points. Don't let your life be ruined by envy and jealousy, Janet. Especially when there's no reason for it."

Again, she nodded. There was a reason but she knew there was no point in discussing it. It wasn't anything that could be changed.

Both her parents hugged her tightly before she went to her room. She was huddled in her bed feeling about as low as she had ever felt when Michelle appeared in the doorway.

"Janet?"

"Yeah?"

"Can we talk?"

"Sure."

Michelle sat cross-legged on the end of Janet's bed.

"I didn't know you hated me so much," she said. The room was quite dark but Janet could tell her sister had been crying.

"I don't think I do hate you, Michelle. There isn't anything about you to hate. Dad hit it on the head. It's all been jealousy and envy. It's not your fault that you're you and that I'm me. Crazy mixed-up genes. Like you got all the good ones and I got what was left."

"But it really isn't that way, Janet," Michelle said. "I've spent plenty of time being jealous of you."

"You don't have to say that just to make me feel good."

"I'm not. You're an interesting person. So funny and imaginative and you can keep people in stitches without even trying. I don't know why I'm like I am . . . why I feel I have to look and act just right and why I worry so much about what people think. I wish I could be more like you and just feel so free and easy but I can't and—"

"You're not missing much," Janet broke in, with a laugh that came out like a croak.

"And you're wrong about boys," Michelle continued. "Lots of them like you. I've dated lots of guys and—"

"And you always dump them like you dumped Steve. You

don't even know what rejection is,'' Janet remarked wistfully.

Michelle gave a short, mirthless laugh. ''I always 'dump them,' as you call it, when I see what's going on. I'm not like you. I can't keep guys laughing and interested. When I can tell they're getting bored with me, I break things off before they get a chance to. But I didn't mean to talk about me. I'm not saying it to make you feel good. It's the truth. Lots of guys have said they really like you. Okay, so Mark was a rat. He's a drip, anyway. But it wasn't that way with Johnny. He came to me very upset, Janet. He really did. He wanted you back and you wouldn't give him a chance. Well, maybe I've been sorry at times that things didn't work out between Steve and me. He's a really great guy. One of the nicest I've ever known. But he likes *you*. Not me. Open your eyes, give him a chance, and you'll see that. Everyone else does. Everyone but you.''

Janet wanted to believe that. She couldn't. It just didn't seem possible.

After a long silence, Janet said, ''I'm sorry I sounded off. Maybe it's not been all bad that it happened if we can get on better terms now.''

''Then you don't hate me?''

''I don't hate you. I really don't. Maybe I'd like you better if you had warts on your nose but . . .''

Michelle giggled. ''With hair growing out of them?''

''Preferably. Listen, though, I want you to promise me something.''

''What?''

''That you won't tell Steve how I feel about him.''

''Janet . . .''

''Please. Just promise.''

''That's dumb.''

Janet replied, ''I won't argue with that. But I still want you to promise.''

''Okay.''

"Thanks."

"Janet?"

"Yeah?"

"It's been a pretty rough night. Would it bother you if I slept in here?"

"No. Not at all."

Michelle slid in under the covers beside Janet. They talked for a while about all sorts of things. It was something they used to do a lot, but it hadn't happened for a long time. For too long. They talked until their voices grew sleepier and sleepier.

"Michelle, you really think Steve likes me . . . as a girl, I mean?"

No answer came. From the other side of the bed, the sound of breathing was deeper than it had been. Michelle had drifted off to sleep. Janet lay there in the dark silence. What would happen next? She wished she knew.

Chapter Twelve

"I can't go through with it. No way. I simply can't."

Janet and Steve stood in the wings out of sight. Six of the most graceful girls in Barkley High were out on the stage performing a jazz dance routine.

"We *have* to," Steve said simply. "We're right after this act. The M.C. will be introducing us in just a few minutes."

"Steve, honest, I can't. I think I'm going to throw up."

Her plea must have sounded sincere because he quit his own nervous fidgeting to look closely at her. He gave her a lopsided grin.

"Even with all that makeup, you're so pale it makes your freckles stand way out. Like three-D all across your nose. This is supposed to be a *fun* act. You can't go out there looking like you're about to be shot."

"What do you propose to do about it?" she asked dryly.

Without warning, he leaned toward her and pinched both of her cheeks vigorously.

"Ouch!" she exclaimed, pulling back out of reach. "What was the point of that?"

"To put some color in your face. Just trying to be helpful."

"Don't bother. The last thing I need at this point in my life is *your* kind of help."

The recorded song to which the girls were dancing reached the last chorus. Janet looked at Steve, shook her head dubiously, and swallowed hard.

"Lindquist, at this moment, will you give me answers to some things I've always wanted to know?"

"Now?" she asked, her voice rising in near panic. "Right *now* you have questions?"

"Yes, I want to know how many football players it takes to change a light bulb. And when you answer that, I want to know if that dress you have on is made out of polyester. Then, when you've explained all that, tell me if you ever learned how to shimmy like your sister Kate?"

Janet giggled. The tension was broken. She could hear the applause from the audience and the six girls in their sequined outfits came back through the curtains. Even though she could hear the M.C. cracking corny jokes and preparing to introduce their act, the butterflies in her stomach had miraculously quieted down.

In a stage whisper, she said, "Number one, if you can't figure out how many football players it takes to change a light bulb, then you're hopeless and there's no point in talking about it. Number two, I wouldn't be caught dead in polyester. Not even at a dumb event like this. And as for your last question, you bet I can shimmy like my sister Kate. *Better.*"

His grin grew wider. "Then it's time to prove it, kid. We're on."

The familiar music filled the high school gymnasium. Just as they had done over and over again during practice sessions, they made their entrance through the curtains. The bleachers and folding chairs were filled with students, parents, and other townspeople, but Janet wasn't really aware of them. Or maybe she was. She was expected to show off and give them a good time and that was what she was going to do. Steve and Janet made their funny faces and exaggerated movements. It was a comedy act but it was also a piece of excellently choreographed dancing. Watching Steve spurred her on to make her own part as lively as possible. The first burst of laughter and spontaneous applause from the audience brought out the ham in her. For the remainder of the routine, the act was a combination of polished choreography and impromptu clowning. They were wild and funny and the onlookers loved every minute of their performance.

Too soon, Janet and Steve finished dancing and left the stage, but the applause continued. The drama coach who had helped organize the project gave them a big grin and said, "You were a hit. You're going to have to take another bow."

"Oh, gosh, no," Janet protested.

"Oh, gosh, yes," the teacher teased.

Taking Janet's hand in his, Steve said, "Come on, kid, when you've got it, you've got it. Don't fight it. Our public awaits us."

Not letting go of her hand, he pulled her back through the curtain. They stood there together, hand in hand, the tall, good-looking boy in the striped jacket and huge bowtie and the petite girl in the tiered pink dress that stopped above her knees, the long string of beads, and the curling hair held back by a twenties-style band. She looked at Steve and grinned. Perspiration was rolling down his face and she could feel a similar dampness on her own. She realized that her heavy stage makeup had probably smeared and looked terrible, but she didn't care. She loved the applause and the glory and she loved Steve.

They bowed deeply toward the audience, danced a few impromptu steps, then blew kisses out toward the crowd before they left the stage again.

When they were back in the wings, the drama coach shook her head, then gave them brief hugs. "I've never seen two bigger hams but it worked. They loved it. Judging from that last routine you obviously had worked out, you must have known you'd get that curtain call."

With that comment, she went on to oversee some scenery changes, leaving Janet and Steve alone.

"It was weird," she said slowly. "We hadn't thought about having to go back out, let alone *practicing* for it like Mrs. Mallory thought, but it was like I knew what you were going to do and you knew what I was going to do. Weird."

"You can say that again. Just think . . . I've been around you so much we're on the same wavelength. That gives me something to think about, Janet."

"I'll bet it does." She giggled, feeling giddy now that the long-dreaded ordeal was over. She had hated it, fought against doing it, and ended up having a great time. Life was difficult to figure out. "If you think you're developing a mind like mine, you better run for your life."

His expression changed suddenly. "I don't think I want to. I *like* your mind."

"Yeah, but you like pizza, too . . . That doesn't mean you want to *be* one," she quipped.

He laughed and the dreamy quality that had been in his eyes was gone. Without thinking, Janet reached up to his face and dabbed at the perspiration that was rolling from his forehead onto his cheek.

"Got a bit warm, didn't it?" he asked softly. With his index finger, he traced a line under her eyes, then pulled back to show it to her. Its tip was black from the mascara that was smearing around her eyes. At the insistence of Michelle and Mrs. Mallory, Janet had allowed the exaggerated makeup of jet-black mascara and bright-red blush and lipstick.

"I better go scrub this junk off and change my clothes. If I try going home like this, people will think I'm a clown who escaped from the circus."

"Hey, look, when this is over, why don't we go get something to eat? I'm starved. I was too nervous to eat dinner before the show."

Janet raised one eyebrow. "Steve Wayman, the great football player, was nervous about something as minor as doing the Charleston?"

"Honey, I'd rather try to recover a fumble any day than dress up like this and dance in front of a bunch of people. Now, you going with me? Michelle can take your car home or I'll bring you back here to get it after we eat."

Janet considered the matter. Actually, there was no reason *not* to go. Now that she and Michelle had straightened things out, all the tension and hostility Janet had felt was gone. She was happy that she and Steve were friends again. Still, she couldn't help wishing that there was more to the relationship than friendship.

"Okay," she agreed. "Let's change, watch the rest of the show, and then go eat about three pizzas each."

"Three each? Then this had better be Dutch treat. I don't have an endless supply of money, you know."

"Oh, all right," she said, pretending to grumble. "We'll go Dutch. Only suddenly I don't feel quite so hungry. Maybe I can make do on one pizza."

"Spoken like a true tightwad."

When Janet had scrubbed all the makeup from her face and traded the flapper costume for jeans and a blouse, she slipped into the seat next to Steve to watch the rest of the variety show. Maybe her attitude hadn't changed completely. It had definitely improved, however. For when Michelle came out in her lovely blue-and-white gown, Janet felt a glow of pride along with the familiar twinge of envy. Michelle was pretty all right . . . pretty enough to take your breath away. But Janet now realized her own good points. She had the ability to make people laugh and she had used it well tonight. From now on, perhaps she could set her mind to dwelling on what she did have instead of what she didn't have. The sound of the applause she and Steve had drawn was still ringing in her ears strongly enough to enable her to smile and applaud for Michelle and Rod in genuine appreciation for their performance. There wasn't any point in trying to compare her act to her sister's. They were too different and that didn't mean one was better than the other.

Later, when she and Steve were seated across from each

other in a booth at the pizza restaurant, she looked at him and gave a long, thoughtful sigh.

"You know what?"

"I know some whats. Probably I don't know all whats. Which what did you have in mind?"

"It just suddenly came to me that it's probably really a blessing Michelle and I aren't alike. The 'sibling rivalry,' as you once called it, has been bad enough as it is. Can you imagine what it would be like if I tried to be like her and entered all the same contests and joined all the same organizations and ran for all the same offices? We'd probably kill each other. Maybe it's a good thing the family genes got mixed up."

"Congratulations, Janet," Steve said softly. "You're finally beginning to use your head for something besides a hat rack."

"Clever comment but not very appropriate. I never wear hats."

"Shall I get you one?"

"Don't bother. Knowing *your* taste, I'd end up with something pretty bizarre-looking. I guess I'll just keep wearing this red stuff that vaguely resembles hair on my head and leave the hats to someone else."

Steve glanced at the mass of shining, unruly curls. "Red? I thought you were a strawberry-blonde."

She shrugged. "That's back when I was five feet eight inches tall. I told you . . . I'm accepting my genes for what they are."

"Nothing wrong with that. You're a little on the messy side, of course, but that's no real problem."

"Messy?"

"You have cheese on your chin," he said, laughing.

She shook her head slowly. "Some things never change."

"I'm not complaining." With that remark, he leaned across the booth and removed the string of mozzarella from her chin with his lips, then kissed her softly on the mouth.

Feeling suddenly shy, Janet didn't know what to say.

There was a long silence which she found somewhat awkward. Steve didn't say a word. He just kept looking at her in a strange way. At last Janet thought of something to say.

"We were really a hit tonight, weren't we, Steve? Gosh, I couldn't believe how much they seemed to enjoy it."

"Yeah, well . . . we're a pretty great team. Seems a shame to break it up."

"But there isn't that much call for Charleston performers in Barkley."

"True, but we could go on to bigger and better things. Like the prom."

Janet stared at him. She wasn't sure she had heard correctly.

"Pardon?"

"The prom," he repeated.

"What does that have to do with anything?"

"I'm asking you to go with me."

"But that's four or five months off yet."

"I know. I just wanted to ask you before someone else beat me to it."

Janet looked out across the restaurant. "Yeah, there is quite a crowd lined up waiting to ask me."

"So what's your answer?"

He looked quite serious. Janet felt uneasy and a little suspicious.

"You don't have to do this, you know. Has Michelle talked to you about me? I mean, since that night I acted weird and ran off?"

He looked puzzled. "Talked to me? Well, some, I guess. Not about you, if that's what you mean. Why?"

One piece of pizza remained on Janet's plate. Suddenly she had no appetite.

"I just mean you don't have to be nice to me. I really don't mind not going to proms and stuff. It's not important."

"But it's *my* senior year," he said, "and it's important to me. So?"

"I don't know what to say," she said slowly. "Right now

you think that because you liked Michelle and she threw you over that you won't like another girl by then so you ask me because I'm your friend and that way you'll be sure to have someone to go to the prom with. But by May, Steve, that may change. I mean, you may like someone by then and . . ."

There was a funny look in his eyes as he stared at her. "I do like someone, Janet. I've liked her for a long, long time. And I just asked her to go to the prom with me. I kept waiting and waiting for some signs she liked me but nothing happened and I got tired of waiting. So I just decided to take the big step anyway."

Janet looked down at her hands. She looked at the piece of pizza on her plate. She looked at the people in the next booth. She looked at the jukebox. She looked everywhere but at Steve Wayman's face.

"Steve . . ." she began, still staring down at the table.

"I like *you*, Janet. In fact, I love you."

Slowly she raised her eyes to meet his. If ever there was a time for honesty, it was now. "But I thought you were crazy about Michelle. I thought you kept hanging around because of her, that you were hoping to get her back. You say you love me, but what happens if she starts showing an interest in you again?"

Steve met her gaze directly. "I started hanging around because of your sister. I don't deny that. The important thing, though, is that long after I got over her, I kept coming around because of *you*. You should believe in yourself, Janet. You're a really great person. That is, when you let yourself be known."

Eyes shining, she said, "I'm not sure I believe this is really happening to me."

"Does that mean there's a chance you like me back?"

"Steve Wayman, I've loved you for ages and ages."

"Then you'll be my girl?"

"I'll be your girl."

"I love you, Janet." Then, right there in the middle of the

restaurant, he leaned across the table and kissed her again, this time in a way that sent shivers up and down her spine.

"You know, Steve," she said when she could breathe again, "I might be a hamburger on life's menu, but there are lots of people who prefer hamburger to cherries jubilee. At least, for a steady diet."

"Lots of people?" he asked. "Some girls get conceited pretty fast. Just remember who's at the head of the line. The hamburger line, if that's the way you want to think of it."

"I'll remember," she said quickly, reaching across the table and giving his hand a squeeze.

"And if you get spacey and forget, I'll remind you. Ready to go?"

A glow began inside her and spread until it lit up her face. "I'm ready," she said softly, sliding out of the booth. Steve held her hand as they walked out of the restaurant and toward his car.

She was so happy. She was in love! And she didn't care who knew it. She wanted to shout it to the world.

Outside, Steve held the car door open for her. "Hey, you know," he said, "we ought to think about doing another routine for the spring talent show." He bent and softly kissed her lips. "But they'll have to place us last on the program. You're a hard act to follow."

Janet looked wonderingly into his shining blue eyes. Oh, yes, she thought, this time she wanted to shout it to the world!